AFTER DELORES

a novel by Sarah Schulman

T0155080

Arsenal Pulp Press  Vancouver

AFTER DELORES
Copyright © 1988 by Sarah Schulman
Introduction copyright © 2013 by Sarah Schulman

SECOND PRINTING: 2022

Arsenal Pulp Press edition: 2013
First published by E.P. Dutton, 1988

All rights reserved. No part of this book may be reproduced in any part by any means—graphic, electronic, or mechanical—without the prior written permission of the publisher, except by a reviewer, who may use brief excerpts in a review, or in the case of photocopying in Canada, a license from Access Copyright.

ARSENAL PULP PRESS
Suite 202–211 East Georgia St.
Vancouver, BC V6A 1Z6
Canada
arsenalpulp.com

Lyrics from "Bad Girls" by E. Hokenson, B. Sudano, D. Summer, and J. Esposito. Copyright © 1978 by Sweet Summer Night Music, Rick's Music Inc., and Earbourne Music.

Excerpt from the poem "Of Mere Being" by Wallace Stevens reprinted from *The Palm at the End of the Mind* by Wallace Stevens, edited by Holly Stevens, Alfred A. Knopf, Inc., publishers. Copyright © 1971 by Holly Stevens.

Excerpts Patti Smith reprinted from *Babel*, Putnam Publishing Group. Copyright © 1974, 1976, 1977, 1978 by Patti Smith.

Lyrics from "Can't Help Falling in Love" by H. Peretti, L. Creatore, and G. Weiss copyright © 1961 by Gladys Music.

This is a work of fiction. Any resemblance of characters to persons either living or deceased is purely coincidental.

Cover photograph: Nan Goldin, "Empty beds, Boston" (1979); Cibachrome, 30 x 40 in (76 x 102 cm)
Author photograph by b.h. Yael
Book design by Gerilee McBride

Printed and bound in Canada

Library and Archives Canada Cataloguing in Publication

Schulman, Sarah, 1958-, author
After Delores / Sarah Schulman.

First published: New York, Dutton, 1988.
Issued in print and electronic formats.
ISBN 978-1-55152-515-0 (pbk.).—ISBN 978-1-55152-516-7 (epub)

I. Title.

PS3569.C5393A47 2013   813'.54   C2013-903261-4
                                               C2013-903262-2

MIX
Paper from
responsible sources
FSC
www.fsc.org   FSC® C103214

INTRODUCTION TO NEW EDITION

Here and Yet, Not There
Sarah Schulman

"Hilarious ... Hard-core. Makes *Bright Lights, Big City* and *Less Than Zero* seem thin and dated." —*Publishers Weekly*

After Delores came out of a vibrant, intense underground of gay women who, in the 1970s and 80s, had been rejected by their families and contexts but refused to give up their homosexuality. There were all kinds of prices one paid for refusing to be subdued; they included poverty, marginalization, and a raw danger that comes into focus when all protections are withheld. There was a physical danger from living without visible ownership by men. Walking down the street alone or with other women, having women coming in and out of each other's apartments, not having access to men's money and prestige—all of these anti-social actions telegraphed a vulnerability to exploitation, violence, and derision. Punishment from the outside world, whether active degradation or passive indifference, became combined with abandonment by family: the absence of familial love, understanding, interest, support, and material and emotional structure. This produced a kind of desperation, a desire to exist when one was not supposed to, especially on her own terms. There was desperation for money, for a sense of safety that could never be accomplished, for a place of rest that was not possible. And the only moment when recognition held a glimmer was with each other—equally deprived and equally determined. The women who had the integrity to be out enough to live their sexuality paid a price in every other realm of their lives.

I now see how that produced a kind of emotional anarchy. If no one cared about what happened to you, then no one cared about how you acted. There was no one more demeaned in your universe than the other gay girls around you, and so replicating the violations she already experienced from her family, from the movies, from her job, was normalizing somehow. Being unaccountable to another lesbian was perhaps the only dominant culture behavior available. So everyone just stood by and let it happen. They simply didn't believe that lesbians should be accountable for their actions. It's the flip side of exile: anonymity. Families were back in Michigan or Jamaica or the Bronx or Scarsdale, no one who knew you was watching, and the only ones who were didn't matter. And yet queer people always needed each other for love and for sex, and for someone to talk to while everybody else in the world was back home for the holidays. I remember Thanksgiving as the busiest day of the year for gay bars. The level of undeserved emotional punishment experienced by queers created an intensity around existence that the protected could never comprehend. It was from this reality that I wrote *After Delores*.

• • •

"A rare and insightful look into the lesbian mind."

—*New York Times*

After Delores was the first modern lesbian novel to have a rave review in The New York Times, written by Kinky Friedman, a singer with a band called The Texas Jewboys, who also wrote detective novels. The review was titled "She Considered Boys For About Five Minutes," and he compared me to Kafka. With this observation, he simultaneously recognized the quality of the writing while acknowledging how new and unusual the novel's point of view was. This, in 1988, was considered to be a good thing. It was very exciting. For the first time in a long time, lesbian readers learned about a book through mainstream media, and our novels were given a capital L ... for literature. There was a rise in stature, opportunity, respect, and therefore, possibility. The book's recognition inspired the publication of other novels with lesbian protagonists over the next four years, thus expanding American literature's range of character, experience, and perspective. *After Delores* was translated into eight languages and was widely read and shared around the world.

But by 1992, this new open-minded environment for lesbian fiction had come to an end, contained by the vagaries of niche marketing. Rarely again would an authentic lesbian novel be reviewed at such a high level by a straight man; it provided too much legitimacy and was too normalizing. Huge retail chains like Barnes & Noble took books with lesbian protagonists off the fiction shelves and stuffed them away in the "Gay" section.

Unspoken quotas were imposed by mainstream media outlets on how many lesbian books could be reviewed, forcing such books to compete against each other instead of being evaluated on their literary and intellectual merits. All of this resulted in an unpredictable paradigm readjustment where writers were suddenly allowed to be out of the closet personally and still achieve recognition, but only so long as their books did not have lesbian protagonists. And soon novels with lesbian protagonists disappeared from the mainstream, while lesbian authors who did not represent themselves in their books were allowed to thrive. This, of course, produced a chilling effect, in which talented fiction writers became fearful of writing lesbian novels that they saw as unpublishable, and a plethora of MFA programs that quickly became necessary to having a serious writing career were unable to provide lesbian students with support and knowledge to write and publish novels based in universes where the author, herself, could also exist. Today, very few novels with lesbian protagonists are written and only a handful are published by mainstream presses, yet it is much, much easier for lesbians and queer women to be out as editors, publishers, and critics, as long as they don't support lesbian fiction. While lesbian characters exist with more frequency in mainstream books by straight authors, I often do not recognize these characters. We became representable by others, and invisible to ourselves.

Just a word on form. My first novel, *The Sophie Horowitz Story* (1984), was the third lesbian detective story to be published. The first was *Angel Dance* (1977) by MF Beal (a pseudonym, I suppose), followed by Barbara Wilson's *Murder in the Collective* (1984). Our lives were a mystery anyway, so the attraction by early lesbian writers made sense. But the choice of genre reflected a desire to be part of popular culture without giving up the authenticity of suspense and threat and romance and pursuit with which we all co-existed. The prototype, of course, is Patricia Highsmith, in particular her book *The Price of Salt*, the best-selling lesbian novel of all time, published under the pseudonym Claire Morgan. In Highsmith's books (*Strangers on a Train*, *The Boy Who Followed Ripley*, etc.) she told us "who did it" right away; the story lay in the perpetrator's guilt. By the time I got to *After Delores*, the detective format was dark. Not only was I also in the urban world of "noir," but I'd gotten there by escaping from the tyranny of positive images that had started to dominate grassroots feminist publishing at the time. Ironically, it was the mainstream that was allowing the pain and contradiction to show, even more ironically because it confirmed their pre-existing prejudices of lesbians as sinister. So truthful, more complex representations were briefly possible in the mainstream because they misinterpreted our contradictions as signs of pathology and not oppression. Even more "ironically," as lesbian content got pushed out of the mainstream, the field overflowed with lesbian detective novels to the point of banality, because we—ever internalizing how we are viewed in dominant cultur—now believed that we did not deserve literature and allowed ourselves to be contained within a genre that has always been considered second-rate.

So now what?

Today, literally twenty-five years after the book's initial publication, it would be impossible for a novel with a lesbian protagonist who is as honest, irreverent, eccentric, and alone as *After Delores*'s is, to be published by a mainstream press. And yet we must keep writing these novels, because it is only by presenting innovative material that gatekeepers become accustomed to it and eventually let down their guard. I don't want to live in a world in which the majority of lesbian representations are family-oriented, celebrity-focused or (shudder), cutesy. Do you?

1

I WALKED OUT in the snow trying to get away from Delores's ghost. It was sitting back in the apartment waiting for me.

Snow was powdering up the sidewalk, but I'd seen too many winters to be surprised by how beautiful they can be. The sky became sheets of clear plastic that moved alongside me through the streets, turning the city into a night of transparent corridors. I walked through it to a few more beers, different places, and ended up at a big, gay dress-up party in the basement of an old public school.

There, the winter night that had been walls turned into men and women dancing together and by themselves and not dancing. One more drink and the skin on my face went numb. Then, for the first time that day, I could relax. That's when I saw Priscilla. Some girl was dressed up as Priscilla Presley in a long black wig and miniskirt wedding dress that said, "I'm a slut but I'm really a virgin," just the way Elvis liked it. She was so hot in that dress I surprised myself, watching her sashay around the hall handing out autographed pictures of The King and swallowing Dexedrine. When I caught her watching me, she came in like a close-up and said in the sweetest Texarkana voice, "Honey, take me for a ride in your Chevrolet."

"You look good in that dress," I said.

She was smiling then but I knew she was deadly serious.

"How good?"

"Real good."

It was all happening so quickly I was almost surprised when Priscilla walked me into a chair and pushed her breasts into my face. I slid my hand down the slope of her ass to the mesa that was the top of her thigh, and then pulled on the rubber seat of her panty girdle, letting it snap back with a slap.

Once we were out on the dance floor, it got even hotter. I'd never gotten so hot so fast for a girl I didn't know before. She wrapped me up in her pink tulle veil and I could hear the crinkling of polyster as our bodies rubbed together.

"You really do it for me, Priscilla."

She looked up from her orange lipstick and tons of black eyeliner, smelling cheap like "Charlie" or "Sen-Sen."

"Honey, you got strong arms. My daddy is a military man and I know power when I feel it."

The music stopped, letting everyone mingle again, but now and then she'd look my way and I knew for sure how hot it was going to be.

There were maybe a hundred people there that night, but all

I saw was Priscilla; otherwise I sat in the chair preoccupied, like sleep or just waiting. In that chair I dreamed that all my teeth were falling out into my hands. I kept trying to stuff them back in until I woke up to Priscilla standing over me, red and shaking. Her demeanor was gone. So was her accent.

"That bitch," she said.

"What's the matter?"

I thought she was talking about me.

"That bitch in the leather jacket. That woman fucked me and then she fucked me over and I'm going to give her hell for it right now."

She flicked her bracelets down her wrist in a way that let me know Pris was just an old-time femme. She was ready to walk right up to Ms. Leather Jacket and slap her face, provoking a huge scene. Priscilla's blood was boiling. She stamped her feet.

"Oooooooh, that bitch."

"Pris," I said, getting straight right away. "Before you let her have it, why don't you change out of your costume?"

"Goddamn that bitch, she can't get away with this."

"Pris, darlin'." I put my hands on her shoulders. "Get out of the costume. You'll feel better."

"You think so?"

"Yeah. She'll never take you seriously in a white mini wedding gown. Come on, I'll help you change."

As we slipped into the heatless back room and she took off her wig, I realized that I had better get a grip on my drinking so I wouldn't keep ending up in situations like this one. She stepped out of her dress and left it lying in a heap on the floor. She washed the makeup off her face and put on her real makeup, took off her orange heart-shaped earrings and put on a nice shirt and nice pants. Then she went to tell that girl where to get off.

There was such a general clamor complete with queer goings-on in that room that night that no one noticed at first when Pris began to yell. Once they caught on, though, everyone pulled back and hung out unabashedly watching them go at it for a while. Ms. Leather was squirming, straining like a big dog on a short leash, trying to get the hell out of there. Pris didn't give a shit about what anyone thought of her. She just kept lashing away, not letting up for a second. I could tell from her face it was all rat-a-tat-tat. Some of the dancing fags enjoyed it for the dish effect, while most found the whole catfight rather messy and unfortunate. But I was happy. Something about it was exciting to me. If you waited for the right moment you could eventually get revenge. Before that night, I'd never considered fighting back. I was still afraid of consequences. But I got off on Priscilla's wagging finger, her swaggering shoulders, her mouth moving so fast it flew off her face. She was doing a dance called getting even. It had been a long time since I'd gotten a thing for anyone besides Delores, but maybe Priscilla was a fairy godmother with a bad case of fifties nostalgia. That's when I started thinking that I might have a dress-up fetish. But what kind of girl would want to dress up for me? I could practically come just thinking about that. But she wasn't really Priscilla Presley and that was that.

By the time Ms. Leather had crawled home and the mess was

all cleaned up, I was deep in a dream and stayed there until Pris tapped me on the shoulder and we ended up back in the snow.

"This is a worthless winter," I said. "It doesn't give you anything. Not quiet, not stopping traffic, not everything white. Nothing."

Pris didn't have proper winter boots, so her feet must have been sopping in those thin things with the spiked heels. Still, she enjoyed the sky full of snow, her face shining in the streetlight.

"Delores walked out on me," I told her.

"Let me guess," she said with a Miss Thing tone in her voice. "She hurt you real bad and all you need is someone to take you home and make you feel better."

"I didn't say that."

"You didn't have to." She was clapping her hands, catching the snow. "I'm little and I'm cute and enough women have told me that's *all* they want that I now know that's *all* anybody wants."

"You want a beer?" I asked, 'cause I wanted one myself.

"Buy me a slice," she said, leading me to a pizza parlour run by stoned Arabs with big grins. It was yellow plastic, too much light, with posters of Yemen and grease-stained wax paper everywhere. Under her leather gloves were five long and polished nails on her right hand and three long polished nails on her left. The index and middle were cut, not chewed, to the cuticle.

"Southpaw?"

"I'm a left-handed lover," she said thoughtfully, holding her hand up to the fluorescent light. "When they grow too long, it's depressing since I don't like to go without. But don't get me wrong, I do believe in love." She had a dreamy teenaged smile on her face. "Want to know what I know?"

"Sure." My voice came out like rancid butter.

"Okay, here it is. Priscilla Presley's philosophy of lesbian love. First, mistresses are fine, but when it gets too serious there's only room for one at a time. Two, it's got to be as over in your head as it is on paper. Three, everybody needs time between affairs to remember who they are. See how easy life can be?"

"But Delores left me," I said.

"Yeah, but she's still got you by the balls."

She picked the cheese off her pizza with those cherry red nails, grease dripping all over the floor.

"You're old gay, aren't you, Pris? You believe in honor."

"I never let a man touch me," she said. "And plenty have tried. I take myself very seriously."

I went next door to get a beer and picked up one for her too. Priscilla was some kind of angel with an important message. I had a question to ask her. It was "Is love aways worth it?" But by the time I got back, she was gone. Only she'd left her little black purse sitting lonely there like me on a yellow bucket seat. Inside it was her address book and a gun.

2

THE BREAKFAST SHIFT started at six forty-five but I punched in at seven on a lucky day. It was still dark outside, no matter what time of year. The crew was always waiting in their early morning attitudes.

"You look like you've been screwing all night," said Rambo, leaning against the register in his military pants, ready to start all his bullshit for the week.

"Smile," said Dino every morning, deep-frying bacon for the fifty BLTs he'd make at lunch.

"Come pick out my numbers," said Joe the cook. He was in the kitchen adding sugar to everything because Herbie, the boss, was so cheap he didn't want Joe putting eggs in the meatloaf or using spices. Finally Joe just gave up on flavor and added sugar instead.

Herbie's customers were living proof that you are where you

eat. The breakfast club wasn't too fascinating except for the couple having an affair. They snuck in a few minutes together before work every day, the guy coming in first, staring nervously at his coffee. Then the lady came. Her hair was done up like Loretta Lynn and she always ordered American cheese on a toasted English and a glass of water with a straw. They'd hold hands across the table and say things like, "Did you see Mel Tormé on *Night Court* last night?" Then she'd get in on his side of the booth and I'd leave them alone until seven-thirty, when she went off to work at the phone company across the street.

Every day was the same day. It started with breakfast, which is always simple. Most people want "two over easy whiskey down" or else "scrambled two all the way." You always have to ask them what kind of toast. Then they leave you a quarter because they think breakfast doesn't merit the same tipping scale as other meals. I'd like to remind them that a token still costs a dollar no matter what time you get on the train.

Herbie's mother came in at eleven carrying shopping bags full of discount paper towels, or honey cake left over from her daughter-in-law's party. Herbie could sell it for a dollar a slice. Joe called her "Greased Lightning" because she moved slowly but still managed to steal waitresses' tips right off the tables. If you caught her in the act, she might give it back, but Momma was one of those bosses who hated to see the employees eat because she saw her money going into their mouths. She hated to pay them or see them get tips because somehow that money should have been hers. Her son was the same way, cheap. Herbie claimed that spring started March 1st. That's when he turned off the heat, which drove a lot of customers over to the Texas-style chili parlor next door.

The lunch rush was a blur where I went so fast I'd forget I was alive and would dream movement instead, swinging my hips back and forth around the tables. This was the most fun because of the challenge and speed and the whole crew teaming up together, feeling closer. So it was always a letdown when the place emptied out at two o'clock, because that was it, money-wise, and the rest of the afternoon was going to be a sit-around bore.

By three o'clock the workers got to eat, which meant sneaking around whenever Momma or Herbie would turn the other way and popping something in your mouth. Technically we could have egg salad or French fries, but Joe would pretend he was slicing corned beef for a Reuben and leave a whole bunch on the slicer for us to grab. Then Dino would forget to put away the fresh fruit salad so we could all have a nice dessert. Only Rambo wouldn't play along. He always threatened to turn us in but was too much of a coward. Rambo spent the entire day leaning against the register showing off his tattoos or talking about the latest issue of *Soldier of Fortune* magazine and how he wished he could have gone over to Lebanon or Grenada instead of being stuck back here in the reserves.

Work was so much the same every day and business was so slow that I had nothing to do but read newspapers and after that stare out the window. That's when I would think about sad things. I couldn't help it. So I started drinking with Joe behind the grill. I guess I just needed to sleep for a couple of weeks but I had to go to work instead, so drinking was some kind of compromise between the two. I knew enough, though, to keep in control of things or else the customers looked at you funny, which makes you feel paranoid and pathetic.

In the old days, I would come home from the restaurant and Delores would be there.

"Hi, baby, I missed you so much," she'd say.

I'd put my nose into her neck and say, "Mmmm, you smell great."

"You don't," she'd laugh, that strange Delores way of mocking and loving at the same time. "You smell like eggs and grease." Then she'd kiss me on the face and slap my ass, being silly and mean and cute.

Even after I took a shower, I never smelled as good as she did. I had to settle for being a nicer person and what the hell does that mean?

3

PRISCILLA HAD THE kind of gun you'd expect from Barbara Stanwyck. It was tiny, with a pearl handle, deadly, sleek, and feminine. I knew that if I hung on to it, I would kill someone. Probably myself.

Delores used to carry a picture of Barbara Stanwyck in her bankbook. On the back was a copy of her favorite Stanwyck quote: "My three goals are to eat, to survive, and to have a good coat." But Delores could never remember if it was Barbara the person who said that or whether it was a line from a movie.

Delores was out for the basics but she also liked being around glitz. She only took the kind of work that let you be near fabulous people. I remember one spring I got a job dressing up as a tomato and handing out flyers for a vegetable stand. Not Delores. She got a job calling up presidents of major corporations and asking them how they felt about their Lear jets. Both gigs paid five an hour, but when I was leafleting downtown Brooklyn, she was phoning from an office on Fifth Avenue.

"You never know who you might meet in Midtown," she used to say. "In Brooklyn, you can be pretty sure."

Also, she loved *People* magazine. We used to go out on Sunday evenings to walk around Astor Place, where all kinds of people were on the street selling their stuff. You could buy somebody's shoes off their feet if you wanted to, that's how down and out everybody seemed. Some people would have good spreads of old books or coffee pots and radios that had obviously been freshly ripped off. But some people just had an old shirt or a couple of magazines they found in the garbage. That's where we did our shopping. Delores would buy weeks-old *People*s and some fashion mags for fifty cents, when they cost five times that in the store. Then when we got home, she'd cut out the most outlandish outfits and paste them up on the bathroom wall.

"Isn't that fabulous?" she'd say. "Really fabulous."

Delores's new girlfriend was named Miriam Silverblatt but she changed it to Mary Sunshine when she got a job as a staff photographer for *Vogue*. It looked better in the credits. They met when Delores had a job in the garment district putting electronic price tags on minks.

It took ten hours to tag six hundred coats and by the end of the day you'd throw those coats around like they were garbage. Sunshine came in to take pictures and caught Delores trying on a full-length in the back. Thinking she was a customer going shopping and not a worker being paid six dollars an hour,

Sunshine asked her out for lunch and the rest is herstory. You always fall for someone thinking they're something they're not. Sometimes I think that fashion was made for Delores, because it's so dependent on illusion. The people involved tell useless lies professionally and make money, then buy contraptions and use them to have sex. Sunshine had a loft in TriBeCa, invested her money, and developed a good-sized dildo collection. She wore tweed pants and expensive leather jackets. I know this because I have investigated her thoroughly.

Having Priscilla's pistol in my pocket opened up a whole new world of possibilities. It might be the opening I needed to get Delores to take my feelings seriously. And if she still wouldn't pay attention, I could get even more serious. If I wanted to, all I had to do was go down to TriBeCa one morning, early, when the few remaining truckers were loading up. Then, when Delores and Mary Sunshine stepped out of their industrial doorway, I could blow Sunshine's brains right out of her head. I'd splatter them all over Franklin Street. I'd have to kill myself too, of course, since the world doesn't understand moments when there are no alternatives but murder. People don't see your pain when you are the killer. So I'd blow away my insides and Delores would have to live with that for the rest of her life. I could never shoot Delores. I love her.

There was something so attractive in that picture that I decided it would probably be better to give Priscilla back her gun as soon as possible. I tucked in my shirt and walked over to the address written on the inside cover of her little black book. There was an endless supply of girls inscribed in those pages, each name written in code with one or two asterisks before the exchange, like ratings on a movie marquee. Her apartment building was across the street from The Blue and the Gold, where Delores and I used to play pool every Tuesday night. We'd stroll over there together and put our quarters down. Delores was a mean pool player from lots of years of hanging out with a wide variety of lowlife. I wasn't bad myself, from a couple of years of hanging out with Delores.

I don't own a television or anything like that, so we'd watch TV there, Tuesdays. In the summer, they had air conditioning sometimes too. Delores never knew what to order so she'd usually take a beer until I made her try a White Russian, then she usually took that. But she never understood about picking the right drink for the right weather. I like bourbon in winter, but summer's right for gin and tonic or white rum and Coke. The rum makes you relax but the Coke makes you wake up, so you get drunk and excited at the same time.

Delores moved out about a month before the night I got a gun. She had cut out on a Thursday and the next Tuesday I went over to The Blue and the Gold secretly hoping that she would show up too and we could get back together. I was sipping my drink and watching the television when Delores walked in all right, but with Sunshine right behind her. They pranced around like a movie mogul and his aging starlet. I know they did that just to spite me, to make sure I got the message that Delores didn't care. Sunshine could have taken her anywhere in New York City and charged it on her American Express card. The Blue and the Gold only takes cash.

After I spotted them, I sat still for a while trying to decide what to do. I could do nothing or I could start screaming in everybody's face. That's something I've considered seriously ever since I was a kid: jumping up and screaming in the most inappropriate places. But when I opened my mouth, the words came out in a thin, whiny string of spit.

"*Delores!*"

She didn't say anything but she did look at me.

"*Delores.*"

"This is a public place," Delores said. "You can't control who comes in here. You're a control freak."

She was doing that fanatic bit where she opens her eyes real wide and pretends that means she's right.

"Look, Delores, if you had busted up somebody's family, would you impose yourself on their party?"

"What party?" Delores asked. "Who's having a party? I don't know what you're talking about."

She started picking her teeth.

"Look, Delores, put yourself in my shoes. Don't you think you would feel bad if you were me?"

"No," she said. "I wouldn't care."

So I tried to man-to-man it with Sunshine.

"Look, Sunshine, you took away my girlfriend five days ago. Can't you go somewhere else but my bar on my bar night?"

She didn't even turn her head to talk. She just let moldy growls drop out of her mouth.

"You can't tell me what to do," she said.

That's when I first got the idea to break her face. She broke my home, I had to break her face. She didn't need my bar the way I did. Sunshine had her own TV and her own video equipment. They could make videos of themselves fucking and watch it together on the VCR.

So I'd stayed away from that dive almost the whole of the new year until the night a gun brought me back to Priscilla Presley. I checked out the place across the street and when Pris didn't answer the buzzer, I decided to stop in for a short one. It was worth waiting for Pris to come home so I could get rid of the gun and The Blue and the Gold is as good a place as any to wait. It's one of those bars where everybody is waiting on the same stools every night on the stumble home from work at five to bed at eleven. Besides, I'd never been there on a Wednesday before and there were whole new worlds of television shows to explore.

I was on my second one, staring at the still-blinking leftover Christmas lights, when a female voice came to me from the other end of the bar. It started as a tickle in my ear and then, for a second, I thought someone had the sense to record a quiet rap song, but when she got so close I could see her reflection in my ice, I realized that a real person was talking to me. A blonde.

"Hey," she said, pulling up a barstool. "You want to buy a phone machine for ten dollars?"

4

WE DRANK FOR a while until the girl asked if I wanted to see the machine. I was tired and needed to talk, so I just decided to tell her the truth.

"I can't. I have to give Priscilla Presley back her gun."

"Do you have to do it right now?"

"I guess it can wait. I'll show it to you if you want to see it, but we have to go into the bathroom."

"No thanks, I've seen guns before. You look kind of sad."

"I am sad."

Somebody played Patsy Cline on the jukebox and that made me even sadder, but in a pleasurable melancholy way, not a painful Delores-type way.

"Look," she said in adolescent earnest as I watched her recite from memory. "You have the possibility to make your life beautiful, but possibility is not forever and it's not immediate.

Know what I mean?"

"Who told you that?"

"Charlotte. That's my girlfriend. So, you want to see the machine or not?"

I paid the check, rang Pris's buzzer one more time, but still no answer.

"She's probably live at Caesar's Palace," I muttered.

"What?" "Never mind. Let's go see the machine."

First, though, the girl had to call her friend who was getting an abortion the next day to see if she needed her to go along or not. It was the last cold night in March and the wind was blowing dark and ugly. She used the payphone on the corner as I huddled in the doorway with a cigarette and tried to push away the tiredness.

"You got your period," she shrieked. "That's great."

The girl seemed only five or six years younger than me but she was from a whole different generation. She wore those black tights and black felt miniskirt and oversized shirt that everybody wore. Her hair was cut short on one side and long on the other with blonde added to the tips. My head was still in the sixties. The only thing that happened in the last two decades that made any sense to me at all was Patti Smith. When Patti Smith came along, even I got hip, but then she went away.

"How did she schedule an abortion without a pregnancy test?" I asked, following her little leather cap and one dangling earring.

"I don't know but she got her period. Isn't that great?"

She started walking east and then more east until it was too east. *There I go again*, I thought, *being old-fashioned*. The idea that Avenue D is off limits was a thing of the past. Now white people can go anywhere.

"Where are we going?"

"Charlotte's place. I have the key."

"How did you know it was okay to come out to me so quickly?" I asked.

"Easy. Charlotte taught me the trick. She says that if you're talking to a woman and she looks you in the eye and really sees you and listens to what you say, then you know she's gay. It works every time."

"Charlotte sounds like a pretty unusual person," I said.

"Yeah," the girl answered, not noticing the cold men in thin jackets, staring silently as we passed by. "Only she's married … to a woman, you know, named Beatriz. I stay at her place sometimes when they've got gigs out of town. Charlotte's an actress. I'm gonna be one too. Beatriz is a director. They're different."

Our conversation was the only sound on the street and her part of it was much too loud.

"It's funny having Charlotte's key. It's like an older person."

"How old is she?"

"Thirty-eight. My father's forty. Why do older people always have keys?"

"Because older people have apartments. They're not moving around staying different places. They know where they live."

"Let's get some beer," she said, heading for the yellow light of a bodega presiding over the steely emptiness of Avenue C. I watched the Spanish men watching her. She was so young. She had no wrinkles on her face and wore a childish blue eyeliner passing for sophistication.

"Let's get a quart bottle of Bud and a small bottle of Guinness and mix it. It's not too bad."

I handed her two dollars over the stacks of stale Puerto Rican sweets and shivered. Even the apartment was cold.

"We make love here in the afternoons while Beatriz is away. Charlotte says she likes the smell of young flesh. She says it smells like white chocolate. Old flesh smells like the soap you use in the morning until it's really old and then it starts to rot. My grandmother used to smell that way but I loved her so it smelled good. One time Charlotte and I came up here and an old man passed us on the stairs. '*I can't stand that smell*,' Charlotte said. '*It's weak and worse than garbage.*' But I was happy because it reminded me of my grandmother. When you love someone, they always smell good. Want to hear a record?"

She was smoking Camels without filters and playing albums by groups I had never heard of.

"Listen to this version of 'Fever.' It's Euro-trash, you know, French New Wave? Instead of the word *fever*, she says *tumor*. 'Tumor all through the night.'"

We sat and listened. My Punkette sprawled out on the floor. Me, freezing in the only chair.

"That was great," she said, pouring more beer. "Let's hear it again."

Her hands were short and white with badly painted black nails.

"I'm so in love with Charlotte," she said.

"How do you know?" I asked.

"Well, she's strong and she's a good lover. You think I'm young but I know the difference. Plus she has good information about life. Like, you know what she told me? She told me to tell all my secrets but one. That way you invest in the world and save a little something for yourself."

She grabbed on to one of the longer strands of her hair and started splitting the split ends.

"I know that she and Beatriz love each other and I'm trying hard to see it from Beatriz's point of view, so that someday we can all be friends. But for now I don't mind seeing her afternoons, I guess. I have to work mostly nights anyway, just a couple of lunches. I go-go dance in New Jersey. I told you that, right? On New Year's Eve, I was so coked up after work and wanted to spend the night with her so badly that I wandered into The Cubby Hole at four-thirty in the morning and they still made me pay."

She had drunk all the beer by that time and smoked all her cigarettes. I gave her some of mine.

"Thanks. There was this yuppie girl there talking to me and I was so desperate I would have gone home with her but she didn't ask. Charlotte encouraged me to take that job, dancing. It's not too bad. Want to see my costume?"

She went into the next room to change and I started smoking. It was so cold. I had on a sweater and two blankets and was still chattering.

"Okay," she shouted from behind the door. "Now sing some tacky disco song."

"Bad girl," I sang. "Talking 'bout a bad, bad girl."

Then she came go-going in her little red sparkle G-string and black high heels. Her breasts were so small that she could have been a little girl showing off her first bikini. She bit her lip, trying to look sexy, but she just looked young. I segued into the next song.

"Ring my bell, bell, bell, ring my bell, my bell, ring-a-ling-a-ling."

"Sometimes they hold up twenties," she said, still dancing. "But when I boogie over to take them, they give me singles instead. 'Sorry, honey.'"

Then I saw her eyes. They were smart. They were too smart for me.

"Charlotte says there's a palm at the end of the mind and it's on fire. What does that mean?"

And I thought, *This kid can get anything she wants, anything.*

She saw me staring at her eyes and got scared all of a sudden, like she was caught reaching into her daddy's wallet.

"I've never done that for someone I respected before."

Those breasts, I thought. *How could anyone make love to those breasts? There's nothing there, nothing at all.*

"Do you think Charlotte will leave her? What do you think?"

"You really believe in love, don't you?" I said.

She looked up at me from her spot on the floor, totally open.

"I don't know what you want from me," I said. "I'm the last person in New York City you should be asking about relationships."

"Do you think she'll leave her?"

Then I realized she saw something special in me. She trusted me. And I was transformed suddenly from a soup-stained waitress to an old professor. We were sitting, not in a Lower East Side firetrap but before a blazing hearth in a wood-lined brownstone. Charlotte was my colleague and Punkette, her hysterical mistake.

"Look, sometimes you have to cheat on your wife and sometimes you have to go back to her."

I looked into her eyes again. They were really listening.

"Maybe you'll get what you want," I said. "But you have to be patient."

And suddenly I wanted her so badly. I wanted to throw off the blankets and be vulnerable again, to roll on the rug with a little punkette in a red G-string and I wanted to show her a really good time. Nostalgia.

5

PUNKETTE HAD MENTIONED a bar called Urgie's in East Newark where she was working nights and some go-go lunches. I telephoned ahead the next day just to be sure and the bartender said a girl fitting that description was working that afternoon under the name Brigitte. I called in sick to Herbie, which wasn't a lie, and decided to go see Punkette dance. The phone machine actually worked so maybe we could be friends.

When the guy started screaming on the subway to Penn Station, I felt for Priscilla's gun in the pocket of my spring coat. When the second guy started screaming in the Amtrak waiting room, I felt it again. The terminal reeked of urine-soaked clothing and roasting frankfurters. It was repulsive. Danger lurked everywhere.

It wasn't until I got on the train to New Jersey that I found Delores's old lipstick in my jacket pocket, which brought back the fact that she still had my keys. Maybe that was a good sign. Across the street from the Newark station was a rundown diner where I stepped in to check myself out in the mirror. Sometimes you just need to know what's going on with your face, to find out for sure what is showing. It was the same old me. I took out Delores's lipstick and put it on real thick until I had a mouth like a movie star—so caked and shiny that no one looks you in the eye. I slipped the gun into my right hand and posed, Wyatt Earp style, in the ladies' room. I wanted to see exactly what Delores would see if I stepped in front of her one afternoon clutching that little piece of metal. Except for the mouth I looked exactly like myself, but happier somehow. And it was all because the machine in my hand could make her shut up and listen for once. Boy, would she be surprised.

It was raining in New Jersey that day, everything typically dismal. The sky was so full of industrial shit and car exhaust, it was all the same color, the color of sweat. New Jersey is a very sweaty state. The only reason girls truck out there to dance anyway is because they don't have to go topless like they do in the city and for the ones trying hard to maintain some distinct sense of limit, it's worth the commute.

Urgie's was a regular place, filled with regular guys from the bottling factory and some construction workers wearing baseball caps. It had fake wood paneling and pink and green disco lights like any tacky family business. Nothing about it was glamorous of half scary. Some of the customers were black, most were white, and three had suits on. They drank beer and ate salami and provolone sandwiches. Everything smelled of yellow mustard. Punkette was right, it's not as bad as they make it out to be.

The stage was also on the tacky side and consisted of a hard plastic sheet laid over the pool table in the center of a circular bar. That way the guys could eat and watch at the same time. After all, they only had an hour. Some girl in a white bikini was dancing around like it was nothing. She had nice legs and smiled a lot, but just a little smile. Every once in a while she'd untie the top of her bra and flash her nipples. Mostly the guys were busy talking and chewing but sometimes they'd look up. Sometimes they'd reach over and give her a dollar, which she'd tuck immediately into her panties. I calculated that if every guy in the place gave her one dollar, it would be exactly the same money as waitressing lunch.

I thought about what it would be like if I started hanging out with Punkette on a regular basis, or eventually got a girlfriend who was a dancer or a stripper. You'd have to stay up late at night keeping an eye out for her and spend a lot of money on cabs. You'd have to bullshit with asshole men all the time and worry about being paid right. That dancer had a smooth belly, but it was flat, not like Delores.

I remember sitting in the bathroom in the morning when she'd come in to brush her teeth. She'd bend over the sink and I'd watch her ass hanging out of her baggy underpants. I loved it so much, I would kiss it. Then, when I took a shower, Delores would come in too. She'd get clean first, but continued to hang out with me in the water so we could both dry off together. What gets me the most of anything is that I really thought Delores was my friend. I thought she'd love me even when she got mad. That's what hurts the most, being violated when you trust someone. Everything gets poisoned.

"Two IDs."

"Excuse me?"

"You gotta be over twenty-one."

The bartender had a tattoo of Andy Capp on his forearm.

"I'm way over twenty-one. Look at these wrinkles on my forehead. No twenty-one-year-old has wrinkles like that. Ask me the jingle of any game show that was on the air in 1960."

"Two IDs."

I dumped the contents of my pockets out onto the bar.

"Well, I don't have a driver's license and I don't have any credit cards. I don't have cards of any kind."

"Then you have to leave."

I stuffed it all back in my coat, leaving a crumpled five lying face up next to the coasters.

"Maybe you can help me. I'm looking for a little girl who works here on and off—blonde tips, red G-string. It's my sister."

He picked up the five and pulled me a draft.

"She ain't here. It's two bucks for the beer."

I put down another five. Didn't get any change. He belched in my face and went off to pour drinks around the bar. I drank down the beer and checked out the dancer. She was probably a psych major from Barnard. Then the bartender came back.

"Hey bartender, you know the one I'm talking about? A punk girl, goes by the name Brigitte?"

"You want another round? Got to keep drinking if you want to sit at the bar."

So I had one more and tipped him three dollars. He started to soften up a bit. This is America, after all.

"Let's see ... Brigitte? Is she the one with the spic boyfriend?"

"I don't think so. She's more the independent type, clear eyes, kind of naïve, but sharp as a fresh razor blade, real hopeful, someone that you'd want to be around."

"Flat-chested?"

"Yeah, that's her."

He wiped the spit off his fat mustache with a mustard-stained bar cloth, leaving a nauseating streak of yellow across his already ugly face.

"She's got a spic boyfriend. He comes in here all the time."

"No, that's not her."

I drank some more beer and tried to decide whether or not to tip the dancer. I didn't want to make her feel uncomfortable in front of all those men, but I did like the way she danced. Plus her cash flow seemed a bit slow. At a particularly dull moment, when I caught a flash of "boy, is this boring" pass across her face, I stretched out over the bar, reached toward the dance floor/pool table, and held out a dollar. Everything kind of stopped. One by one, the guys weren't talking anymore and started paying attention until all you could hear on top of the disco music was the sound of them chewing salami and her feet shuffling against the plastic. But that little darling, bless her heart, gave me a big one-dollar smile, took the cash, and stuffed it into her panties like I was a regular anybody.

Well, I guess a dollar is a dollar, even if it's queer.

It took about thirty seconds for everything to get back to normal and soon the growl of men's voices took over again. That's when it occurred to me that Punkette, being nobody's fool, probably got a better gig in a higher-paying place. She didn't need that dump. If I looked around long enough, I knew I'd run into her again and we could be friends. If she and Charlotte and Beatriz could work out a three-way thing, maybe Delores and me and Asshole could do it too. I was feeling light and ready for one more beer when the bartender came over my way smelling like a rotting Blimpie.

"I'm not running no dating service for you, sweetheart. You're drunk. Now get the hell out of here before I call a cop."

I cursed myself all the way back to the station, getting drenched in the slimy drizzle. That asshole, pushing me around. Everybody's always pushing me around or walking out, or not showing up or somehow not coming through. And I'm the worthless piece of trash that's hurting like hell because of it.

It was just then that I jammed my hand into my jacket pocket and smashed my knuckles on a cold piece of metal. Then I remembered that I had a gun in my possession. I could use it any time I chose. I clutched it first and then tapped it slightly, running my forefinger along its chamber. I knew I didn't have to worry anymore, because the next time somebody went too far, I had the power to go farther. I had a gun. Now everyone had to pay attention. Nothing bothered me for the rest of the afternoon, as I stepped over the broken concrete, the New Jersey dirt turning to mud. It was the new me. I had Priscilla's gun in my pocket and if I'd wanted to, I could have turned around and shot the eyes right out of that fucking bartender's nasty head. But why use up a good thing? There would be better opportunities later on, and more deserving victims. Besides, this gun was a trump I could only play once.

6

WHEN THE NEWS came the following Wednesday, it came the hard way, during lunch in section two. At first, things were fairly normal. The place was empty until the noon rush brought the operators and the one o'clock brought the lawyers.

None of the phone people actually earned enough to eat out every day, but it was too depressing to eat a sandwich at the same desk you sat at watching your life go down the drain. So they scrimped and ordered a lot of little things, like a cup of soup with extra crackers and a small salad with dressing on the side and tea with extra lemon and water, no ice, which was three trips for me. I often got the feeling that the waitress was the only person in their lives that they ever got to push around, so they took full advantage of the opportunity. Joe always says that working people should help each other out, but the sad truth is that most people never think about who they serve.

They just accept it. But every waitress knows that a lot of side orders is a lot of work.

The lawyers were different. They lived defeats and victories every day, so there was always something to get over or to celebrate. That meant a cheeseburger deluxe, which is one trip and a dollar tip, guaranteed. They'd wolf down the burger and a fattening dessert and then run off somewhere, so you could get two tables of lawyers for the same hour that one of the operators took.

By the time things slowed down on the floor, the guys behind the counter would go crazy with boredom. Joe had been drinking rum for an hour and had already picked out his horses. Rambo and Dino were usually deep in conversation.

"I know you suck dick."

"I do not suck dick. I eat pussy."

"Do you suck ass too, or do you only suck dick?"

"You suck dick, I don't suck dick."

I took a look at Dino's *Daily News*. US ships were firing on the Gulf of Sidra. Reagan said, "I am a Contra," and on page seventeen, next to a Macy's ad, was an old photograph of Punkette. She was standing over a cake, smiling. She was a brunette and her hair was long with little bangs. She wore a gold cross around her neck and too much eye makeup, even then. The caption said her name was Marianne Walker, photographed at her fifteenth birthday party. She had come to New York City from Allentown, Pennsylvania, on the Greyhound bus and she was dead. The article said she'd worked as a call girl and a stripper up until the night that someone squeezed her neck until it broke. Then they dumped her in the East River behind the projects on Avenue D.

I looked at the picture and I just lost it. I lost it so bad I couldn't even walk out of the place. I kept on picking up tables and placing orders. When you hear something too awful like that, your whole body gets frightened. It jumps.

I looked around at the customers pouring ketchup on their French fries and drinking Cokes. Urgie's customers in East Newark were just as tame. They weren't dangerous. They were normal. Punkette wasn't a hooker. The paper got it wrong 'cause it's all the same to them. No one was going to take the time to find out what really happened. People watch real life the way they watch TV, sitting in an armchair drinking a beer and talking during the commercials. They love brutality, it's so entertaining. They hate victims. Victims make them feel weak. But I cared about Punkette and someone else out there did too. Maybe it was the girl on the telephone who didn't need an abortion after all. Or Charlotte, who was almost forty and filled with passion and wise thoughts. I was sure, at that moment, we were all three sad.

After that I wanted a drink, so the second that work was over I headed for the bar. But I couldn't step in the door of The Blue and the Gold. It stank. I found myself walking east again until the dirty bodega shined like a star from the corner of Avenue C just like it did that night with Punkette. I bought a beer and sat on a milk crate in the back, drinking it in the store while the Puerto Rican woman on the register watched TV. I don't exactly understand Spanish, but you get used to hearing it and I could tell what was going on because the emotions were so huge. Men and women in fabulous costumes were fretting, threatening, falling passionately in and out of love. The characters yelled and screamed and cried and danced around. They felt everything very deeply. American TV actors just stare at each other and move their mouths. Sitting there watching those people on channel forty-seven let it all out, I learned something very personal. I learned that sometimes a person's real feelings are so painful they have to pretend just to get by. That's what I'd been doing. When you get hurt and can't trust people, they stop being real. Of all the people I'd been running into lately, Punkette was the most real because, in the middle of a lot of sordid business, she still had faith in love. I could picture her dancing away at Urgie's thinking about Charlotte, glowing. She probably even found something to relate to in that ugly bartender, because she certainly found something to relate to in me. When Delores was home, I loved her every day, even when I was sick of her. Then she changed too fast and I was so used to loving her that I let her get away with it. There was a moment, in the bodega, when I loved Punkette instead, but it was too late for that.

In the back of the store, they had three shelves filled with devotional candles covered with drawings of the saints. I bought one for Saint Barbara and lit it right there. The woman didn't blink. People probably made novenas on the spot every day, next to the cans of Goya beans. On the back of the candle was written

¡O Dios! Aparta de mi lado esos malvados.
O God! Keep the wicked away from me.

I had to laugh at myself, going to all the trouble of praying and then only asking for less of something. I didn't want more of anything, no money or love or sex. I was praying to Saint Barbara to take the pain away. When Punkette died, something changed in me. That's when I decided to have a talk with Charlotte.

7

THE NEXT MORNING I tried Priscilla's one more time. Even though I realized that she was probably crazy as a loon, I had to admire her because she had the courage to live out her fantasy. She wanted to be Priscilla Presley instead of whoever she really was, some word processor named Ann Brown from Cincinnati or the like. So she didn't let other people's opinions stand in the way of her pleasure. Pris was as brave as a drag queen, and just as tough. Even though no one was home, I went back happy Pris was in my life. Then I got ready to meet Charlotte.

I wasn't sure whether it was gift wrap or disguise but I knew to decorate myself for Punkette's lover. I powdered and primped, and put on long dangling earrings with silver filigree. It was almost a party mood, light and dancing, grooving all over the apartment. I was hopeful, like riding the open highway on a motorcycle with your hair streaming out behind you in the hottest heat of summer.

For the last month there hadn't been any clothes in my life, just five days of the same pants, with or without a waitress apron. But that afternoon in early spring, I searched for something pretty to put on my body. Tucked back in a corner of the closet was one of Delores's shirts, overlooked in her last-minute packing. Maybe she'd left it for me as a warning, maybe as an excuse to come back in case she needed one. She probably didn't want it anymore. The material was silky and billowing, the color, a rich teal. In her shirt I looked, all of a sudden, touchable and breezy.

Charlotte's block was different in the daylight. I recognized that particular brand of dingy that's not at all the same as poor. There was a special kind of neglect that felt like sabotage, and a lack of self-love evident everywhere. No mothers yelled to their kids from tenement windows. No music floated down from the lips of thin musicians in crowded apartments. No teenagers cut on the radio to dance and flirt in lots and hallways under the nostalgic eyes of old people in their ancient folding chairs. No. Too many junkies had taken over too much territory. When the sidewalk belongs to the junkies, it lies cracked and bland. When there are people, but no signs of life, the buildings that carry them sag with the loss of expectation.

The lock had been torn off the front door of her building, a sure sign of rooftop shooting galleries. The stairs were covered with burn scars from men and women nodding out, cigarettes hanging from their mouths, then dropping to the floor with spit. I hadn't seen any of it with Punkette. The night was too cold and I was too drunk. Two skinny teenagers in oversized jackets passed me on the stairs discussing crack hits, three for ten. A woman in tight pants, holding a large-sized bottle of Pepsi, let herself into an apartment, leaving behind the stench of menthol cigarettes.

I knocked at Charlotte's door and waited, then knocked again. The only sign of life came from the neighbor two doors down, who was busily installing a conspicuous contraption onto his front door.

"Excuse me, do you know Charlotte?" I asked.

"Hold this, will you?" he said, talking me over to his side of the hall, where I pressed two pieces of metal against the door.

"Putting in a new lock," he added, grimier than this job suggested. "They came in through the window the first time so I had to put in bars. Then they walked in through the front door. Try that again, cocksucker. See, all you have to do is tamper with the door and there's a little shock in store for you."

He waved me away without looking in my direction, flicked a switch inside the apartment and I jumped back as a sudden sharp vibration buzzed through the door, followed by an equally sudden silence.

I knocked at Charlotte's door with a little more urgency, ready to get away from that guy. Her peephole was blocked with a matchbook cover, taped from the other side. When I looked through it, I could make out the words *You too can get a high school equivalency...*

"She's probably at the theater," he said in a wasted drawl.

This time he turned and faced me, so I had to look at him more closely and saw a wild mustache and bushy old-fashioned sideburns, like an antique image from a sixties album cover. He wore a torn, stained, leather-fringed cowboy jacket, the kind that hadn't been around for a long time until yuppie stores started carrying them in purple suede for girls. He had these shit kickers that were too heavy for the weather and too redneck for the territory. They were boots that could really kick ass and weren't good for much else besides attitude. This guy wasn't a leftover hippie. He was more Hell's Angels without the colors.

"Which theater?"

"Where they work. A few blocks up the avenue, next to Cuchifritos. Want a lift? I'm taking my cab out in a minute."

I've trained myself to avoid all potentially unpleasant situations with men even though I walk into them constantly with women. Once I realized women could be pretty nasty, I actually considered boys for about five minutes until I remembered that they bored me very quickly, and if someone you love is going to bring tragedy into your life, you should at least be interested in them. So my "No thanks, I'll walk" was part routine behavior and part deliberate avoidance.

The theater was a boarded-up storefront on the ground floor of a tenement. It was quite large and long for what it was and had very low ceilings. You could tell it had once been an old-time bakery because the oven marks were still visible, scarring the worn-out brick walls. I came in quietly through the front door, which opened into the back of the audience area. There were soft lights up on the playing space, where two women seemed to be involved in a rehearsal. The one onstage was very tall, especially against the low ceilings. Her skin was the palest white and she was draped in soft black clothing that made her comfortable and classical, like the beautiful woman in a wine commercial stepping out of her lover's bed in the morning wearing his coziest sweater. It made you want to watch her. Another woman was sitting with her back toward me. All I saw were her curls of brown hair. She was watching too and taking notes as the actress recited her lines.

"I used to babysit for this family over by where the main road is before they put in the highway. I was babysitting for their son and afterwards, Allen, that was the father, he would drive me home. Sometimes, though, we stopped off at Nick's for cheeseburgers and played the jukebox. I liked being out with a grown-up man. It made me feel sexy. Anyway, one night, instead of driving me home, I just sat around in the living room and talked with him and his wife Jackie. And then they talked me into bed with them. So that's how it went. After babysitting, I would go to bed with them. Only I would never let Allen put it in. The thing that used to kill me was when I would make love with Jackie and he would screw her right in front of me. I hated it. I would sulk the whole way home in the car. I started going over there in the day when I knew he would be off working. Jackie was usually reading or in the garden. We'd chat, but nothing happened. Finally one afternoon she said to me, 'You know, I thik you're a lesbian. You'd better not come round here anymore.' They moved soon after that."

It was only when she finished that I remembered it wasn't real. I felt like a spy in a private conversation, and when the conversation was over, I had a stake in it. When the actress dropped her hands and stood quietly onstage, I missed the character that she had become, and felt sad to watch her disappear. So, I let myself stay hidden there in the shadows, waiting to be thrilled again.

"That was shit," said the curly-haired woman.

"Fuck you, that was great," said the actress.

"What are you supposed to be thinking about when you tell this nostalgic little story?"

"You know," the actress said. "I'm thinking about being a girl again. I'm thinking about the different ways that women have said no to me ever since I was a girl, leading up to my lover who just threw me out."

"Well, if the events of the night before, the brutality, are not present in the telling, then this monologue has the sentimentality and saccharine sweetness of a greeting card."

"Don't' be a cunt. Do you want me to do it again?"

This provoked the curly-haired woman, who jumped up onto the playing area and yelled, "How did she throw you out?"

I could tell that she yelled that way to get back in control. She wanted the actress to be responding to her, not the other way around. But the actress didn't say a word. She was significantly taller than the director and just looked down at her with a deep tenderness that was so insulting because it was obviously put on. That's when the director reached out with both hands and gave the tall woman a shove.

"Beatriz, don't push me."

"Let me remind you of what just happened, ten short hours before," Beatriz said with a distinctly abusive tone, punctuated by a series of shoves and jabs at the actress's long body. "'Get out,'" she continued, playing it all her way. "'Get out, I don't love anymore.' That's what she said to you, isn't it? 'Get out. I have been trying for the last six months to get your stinking carcass out of my goddamn life. Now, get out.'"

The actress put her hands out to defend herself but she never hit back, either because she was afraid she'd hurt the little woman with the big will, or because she was afraid she'd lose. Beatriz kept telling her to get out.

"'You're so ugly, no one will ever love you.' That's what she said last night, isn't it?"

That's when the actress started to break down, crying within herself at first, like she was trying to hold back, but the tears came anyway and they were followed by absolutely convincing shaking and heaving shoulders. She sank down to the floor and looked up at Beatriz.

"Please let me stay. Please let me stay."

She said it over and over again, faster and faster.

"Please let me stay. Please let me stay. Five more minutes. Let me stay five more minutes."

"Okay," Beatriz said, dropping her arms, absolutely normal again immediately. "That's better. Now, do the scene again."

The actress took her original position and began. As soon as she started, the character that had been talking when I first walked in returned, magically, where a minute earlier she was nowhere to be found.

"'You know, I think you're a lesbian. You're a lesbian. You'd better not come round here anymore.'"

Then, without missing a beat, she jumped out of her character and out of her light, saying, "I'm so fake, I'm so goddamn fake," and punched the air with both fists. The second fist was the moment when she saw me, so she turned my way and spoke again.

"Can I help you?"

This woman had just transformed three ways in one moment. First she had been in character, then she broke it completely, becoming a temperamental actress stomping across the stage. Then she saw me and stopped on a dime. She turned courteous and charming and looked straight into me.

"Can I help you?" she repeated.

That was the first time I saw her eyes.

"Are you here about the job?"

"Yes, that's it."

I didn't know what she was talking about but it was the flash in her eyes that made me want to say yes.

"Great, I'll be right with you."

She wiped her face with a towel and drank seltzer out of the bottle. Beatriz didn't even turn around. She was busy writing. The actress came closer and extended her right hand. It was huge and carved with veins.

"My name is Charlotte. How strong are your secretarial skills?"

"Fair."

I thought she was playing a game, until she looked my way again. Her face was different one more time. She was relaxed and familiar, like my lover, my closest comrade, my dream girl. Then she watched how I reacted. I was getting ready to tell her all about Punkette, that she was my friend and I wanted to find her killer, but before I could figure out how to say it, Charlotte handed me a pencil and the backside of an old flyer.

"I'd like you to take some dictation. There's no dictation involved in this job but I just want to see how it goes. Where are you working now?"

"Herbie's Coffee Shop. Downtown. Three days a week."

She seemed to like me even though I gave her no reason to. Maybe it was Delores's shirt. I'd never worked clerical before. I always figured that if you went in for typing you'd end up a typist, and I didn't want to end up that way.

"I'll give you some sentences and you take them down."

"Okay."

"Number one. 'My last lover's name was ... ' Fill in the blank."

I wrote "Delores."

She looked over my shoulder, smelling sweaty like a man.

"Where is Delores now?"

"She left me for Nelson Rockefeller."

"I see." She was prim and business-like. "Number two. 'We will all go to heaven for this.'"

I giggled.

"Number three. 'When I laugh like that, I feel ... '"

"Nervous."

She took the paper and looked it over very carefully. I wanted to bring up about Punkette but I just couldn't. I couldn't disappoint Charlotte. I didn't want her to think that I had lied about the job. I could get in touch later and explain everything.

"Thank you very much."

She held out that hand again.

"If you don't get the job, I hope you will come back and visit."

And then she smiled the sweetest smile.

8

I DON'T LIKE to admit it but women are the worst tippers. They put their heads together to divide up the bill and actually figure out exactly fifteen percent without taking into consideration how much they made you run around. Men don't talk about it. Each one peels a dollar off his billfold and quietly leaves it by the side of his plate.

It was a tough day at Herbie's because Momma was ragging on all of us. Joe and I were drinking rum, trying to stay out of her way. Some cooks make you feel tired, others are plain annoying, but Joe charmed me somehow into being more feline. With gold chains shining on his brown skin and a toothpick hanging from his lips, every favor he asked was a service, and his smile, approval. The way he'd say, "Got it, babe," when I called in my order, no matter how busy he was, always reminded me that he was my pal.

"Rum is good," he said in his Caribbean accent, "but it can betray you. When you get the shakes, you've gone too far. Don't go that far, you're still a lovely girl. You're a sweetheart."

Then he looked both ways and poured some more into my coffee cup.

"But," he sighed. "What can you do? The world is so full of pain."

Then he'd scratch his big stomach and laugh.

"I'm going home to Brooklyn and smoke some cocaine and turn on the television. Oh, I'm getting fat from all the sugar in the soup."

When Joe left, I hung out with Dino, who was on the grill until closing. He was telling his war stories again because there was nothing at all happening on the floor.

"I was all over the Pacific during the war," he said. "They sent me to islands I didn't even know the names of till I was on 'em. Then we got two weeks of R and R in Hawaii. That was nice. Hotel, everything."

"Did they have segregated regiments then, Dino?"

"Yep. And drill sergeants of both colors. All of them ugly as homemade soup. Oh-oh, check out Rambo. Thinks he's so sly, that jerk."

Rambo was busy being the big man and giving away food for free to a cute Puerto Rican clerk from the hardware store. She was playing coy and hard to get. But Rambo had picked the wrong moment to get off the register, because the place was too empty and Momma was keeping her eye on everything. That's when I realized that for all his tough-assed talk, Rambo didn't even know how to steal and get away with it. He was putting on his whole show right out in the open, wildly flagrant without choosing to be.

"That turkey is so overt," Dino said.

Rambo ran rampant all over the kitchen. He whipped up a plate of the rarest roast beef while Dino sat there chuckling and covering his eyes. The slices were so red and bloody that Momma could spot them from a block away.

"Thief," she shrieked, with a shrillness that made the orange wallpaper tremble.

"What's the matter, bitch?" he said under his breath.

"Do you have a ticket for that? Where is the ticket? Thief, you steal the food out of my mouth.

"Fuck you, twat," he was screaming all of a sudden. He was screaming louder than she was. "Fuck you and your dead meat."

"Get out of here," she yelled. She yelled but she didn't move, like she had been firing people from that chair for forty years. Taking someone's job away involved such a natural sequence of events for Momma that it didn't require any energy anymore. Rambo picked up the roast beef and smashed it against the wall, which broke the greasy mirror. Up until that point it had been pretty interesting, but I didn't like it at all when the mirror cracked. A curse by Rambo would be hard to shake.

"I'm gonna kill you, you bitch. Watch your ass. I'm gonna kill you."

But he didn't kill her. He just walked right out the front door. The clerk from the hardware store kept sipping her 7-Up as though she didn't care about anything one bit. Me and Dino stood there without making a move. I did not want to touch that meat, lying in the crud on the restaurant floor, but I knew it would be me.

"Come on," Dino said. "I'll help you."

He started picking up the pieces of plate and beef and putting them in the garbage. Momma walked over, real slowly, watching us like we had been the ones who broke it.

"Dino," Momma said. "Those garbage bags cost thirty-five cents each. Don't use so many. Smash the garbage down with your feet. Don't be lazy. Be strong."

"I'm not lazy," Dino said calmly.

"And you," she said, pointing to me. "Find a doctor with a good practice and everything will be under control."

"That woman loves money," Dino said after she waddled away.

"She called you lazy."

"Don't pay her no mind. She loves money too much."

He picked out a penny from the garbage.

"I'll give this to Momma. Then she'll be happy." And he smiled at me. "Don't let it get to you, there are beautiful things in life."

But for some reason, I just started crying and crying.

"You got to get a grip on that drinking," Dino said.

9

HERBIE'S COFFEE SHOP was in the same neighborhood as Sunshine's loft. That's how I knew so much about her. She used to come in for breakfast with various models she'd picked up on shoots. They had to eat at Herbie's because all those Yup-Mex, blue-margarita places don't open until lunch. Sunshine was one of those customers who never thought their waitress was real, never recognized her, never learned her name. She'd leave the coffee sitting there while she made witty conversation and then called me over to complain that it was cold. Some afternoons I could see her and Delores whiz by on Sunshine's motorcycle. They were so cool, I could throw up. TriBeCa was exactly where they belonged. There were a lot of offensive people living in TriBeCa, which was, in general, an offensive neighborhood. And in relation to those kinds of people, I was their servant.

There were still a couple of artists living around that area, but only the rich ones. There was one in particular who was very famous. His picture was once in *People* magazine. He used to come in and talk about money for five to six hours at a time. He was always surrounded by people who said yes to everything he said, and he talked so loudly you could hear him in any corner of the restaurant. One day he was talking loudly again, as usual.

"I've just returned from my Eastern European tour where I developed great insights into the difference between communism and capitalism."

Just then Charlotte walked into the restaurant and took the table right behind the artist.

"Under capitalism, a family living in Harlem will never see Paris. Under communism, a family living in Budapest will never see Paris. But the family in Harlem *might* one day see Paris. And that is the difference."

I was embarrassed that Charlotte should see me wait on someone so stupid, but when I went over to her, she leaned across the table like a co-conspirator.

"You want to know the difference between communism and capitalism?" she asked.

"Sure."

"Under capitalism, people with new ideas serve people with old ones. Under communism, it's exactly the same, only you don't get tips."

And then I realized that Charlotte had come to see me.

"Did I get the job?" I asked, not knowing whether to laugh or not.

"I have to admit that there is no job. Forgive me?" She kissed my hand.

"Sure." "I do these things," she said, "because I like provocation. Otherwise I'm bored and nasty all day long. Besides, I didn't want to talk about Marianne in front of Beatriz. You understand that, don't you?"

"Yeah, but, how..."

"Marianne told me all about you. She said you were very kind. You paid for her drinks. You shared your cigarettes. You gave her advice and you didn't try to get her into bed. I thought you'd show up eventually. After all, Marianne was a very attractive young woman, wasn't she?"

"Yes, she was."

"But we'll talk more about this later. What time do you get off work?" She sat there for the next forty minutes making friends with Dino and Joe by imitating all the customers. Charlotte was amazing because she could be anybody at any time. She could be whoever you wanted her to be and still have total control of the situation. She was an entertainer all the way.

When work was over, we walked to the park.

"How could you possibly get bored, Charlotte, playing characters all day long?"

"Acting is so great," she said. "I love being hateful especially. It's so satisfying. It's terrible in life but onstage it's the best. That way, everyone watches you more closely and then they want to soothe your sorrows and make you a better person."

As she talked, I could see how smooth she was. She knew

which facial expression to use to communicate every situation. Her face was capable of such refined emotions that she managed to convey what she was thinking and acknowledge what I was thinking and still be polite. But there were always surprises. Like I'd be right in the middle of explaining about Delores when, "Oh, God!"

"What is it?"

"I saw a baby slobbering all over himself. It was great."

She was a kid, ready to grab and respond to anything immediately. She didn't let her life walk all over her.

It was just warm enough in the park to try out a bench. I could feel Charlotte breathing next to me. She smelled like a horse. It was so exciting. Charlotte really felt things, just like those guys on Spanish TV, and it made me a little freer, being near her. My whole body was tingling, my muscles were breathing. No wonder Punkette loved her. Since Delores, I haven't known how to relate to people sometimes because I can't tell how much they really feel. If they pay attention to me, I don't know if they're doing it on purpose or if it's a trick. But, with Charlotte's voice on my neck, I realized how much I had missed closeness. I think I got too turned on, though, and kept interrupting maniacally, for no reason but to be in conversation with Charlotte. To see her teeth.

"Charlotte, when you were little, what did you want to be when you grew up?"

"Growing up has always been an elusive question in my life."

"What does *elusive* mean?"

"Fuzzy, changing shape."

Actually I think I did know what *elusive* meant, but I was so excited that I forgot.

"Let's see," she kept going, "I used to play games all the time. I had six brothers. One died. Three of them are priests. The other—"

"What kind of games? Oh...I'm sorry."

I wanted to shut up. I really wanted to shut up.

"That's okay. Princes and dragons and buccaneers. We would—"

"Princes? Do you want to get a beer? I'm sorry...I am listening. I'm hearing every word you say."

I was. I was listening too hard. So she got silent. Almost sullen. I had no idea at all of what to do until a derelict walked by laughing to himself.

"I don't like homosexuals," he said.

And I loved him for that because he could see the same thing in me that he saw in Charlotte. It put us in the same boat. I wanted her to put her arm around me but instead she flattened her black hair and took off her earrings.

"Better get rid of these and back to my tough self."

Right there before me on a park bench, she transformed from the soft woman onstage, laughing and open, to an Irish butch with a set jaw and big hands, who comes home at night with tight shoulders, needing loving from her woman. I think that was the first time that any of Charlotte's personas struck me as real. She was a woman who wore suit jackets and men's pants. She'd stick her hands in her pockets and clam up when she really had something to say.

She was so close and within reach that I could no longer abide by the rule of touching and not touching. I put my hand up flat against her lapel, in the lightest way, and then pulled back, reaching for a cigarette and offering her one.

"No thanks, I don't smoke anymore."

That's what stayed in my mind all night, tossing and turning on the couch. Charlotte doesn't smoke. How could I ever be close with a woman who doesn't smoke? No bitter taste of tobacco on her tongue when I suck it. No late-night waves of smoke hanging on our shoulders. No red tip smoldering in the dark. No passing the butt from lip to lip. She would never love my smell the way a nicotine addict craved me. That's when I wondered if Charlotte was only my diversion, and I was nothing to her. But that thought was too bleak to possibly accept.

10

I'D KIND OF dropped the idea of giving Priscilla's gun back right away. There's really nothing that strange about having a gun. Most people in New York City seem to have one. It's normal. You're just expected to be cool about it and keep it hidden in a sloppy way. Then everyone knows you have one but nobody ever mentions it, like genitals or money. The truth was that after playing around with the gun so much, and practicing the idea of using it, I was getting used to the thought of shooting somebody.

Murder doesn't have to be a lonely tragedy. Especially in self-defense. I mean, I could kill Delores any day of the week and it would be in self-defense because she was hurting me around the clock. But that type of reasoning doesn't play in the public eye. You can only kill to protect a woman other than yourself if you want to get away with it. That's the trick, I think, that guys often use. They start out wanting to punch anyone in the mouth and then look around for the nearest rude drunk harassing some girl. That way they get their rocks off and can be a hero at the same time.

Let's say one night me and Charlotte would be on the trail of Punkette's killer. All the clues lead to an abandoned shooting gallery between a video store and a *botánica*. It's after midnight and we're picking through the garbage and human shit and used works by candlelight until some big dude steps, suddenly, out from the shadows. He whips out his knife and delivers a speech about why he killed Punkette, including all the practical details. He tops it all off with a sinister laugh and lunges for Charlotte's throat. That's when I'd pull out my revolver and let him have it right in the gut. We'd leave his corpse for the rats and run out, euphoric, onto the street. Charlotte would love me forever for that. She'd throw her arms around me and cry real tears. I'm sure everything would feel better then.

If Charlotte and I were going to find Punkette's killer, we had to get started soon. I hadn't heard from her since that day in the park and it scared me to think she might be slipping out of my life. I couldn't let that happen. I put on Delores's shirt again. There are those of us in this world who understand nothing about clothes, about what looks good and why. When one garment succeeds, it becomes a permanent part of the repertoire, a habitual sure thing. Delores's shirt had worked for Delores and, so far, it had worked for me. Now there were other, more pressing, matters.

It was almost comfortable walking over to the theater. Charlotte's neighborhood and I were getting used to each other, or maybe I was becoming part of it. Some streets in New York City are fab and their people are fabulous too. Some streets are preoccupied and keep to themselves. Some are broken and tired. Some accept things the way they are. Charlotte's streets compose their own universe with their own personal sense of order and not too many questions or possibilities. They're not romantic or inviting but that's why they suck you in. Especially if you're the kind of person who doesn't feel like looking at the future right now.

The front door wasn't locked so I stepped into the theater's cool darkness. Beatriz was there again, alone in the front row. I knew I shouldn't disturb her, because she was busy thinking about something dramatic. And, I probably shouldn't involve her in the Punkette thing, because her feelings must be very mixed. But I was curious about what kind of woman would shove Charlotte around in order to get her to do what she wanted her to and then have it work. Beatriz seemed to be staring at the empty stage. Every once in a while she would make a little sound, a snort of recognition, and then, a note.

"Excuse me."

She looked up, interrupted but smiling graciously. A person with very good upbringing. Diplomatic. Not a common person.

"You are Marianne's friend, aren't you?" That scared me right down to my fillings.

I thought Charlotte didn't want her to know about Marianne. Or was it that Charlotte specifically did not want Beatriz to talk to *me* about Marianne? Did I know something special or had Charlotte changed her mind? I wanted to get out of there but she beat me to it by saying, "Come in and sit down. I've been waiting for you."

She was miles ahead of me and flaunted it with style. She knew more than she should have known but was polite enough to tell me so. Beatriz didn't let suspense hang in the air like the melodrama of a waterfront movie, foghorns and mist. There were no raised eyebrows or padded shoulders and vampire nails. No, she said it like she was really thinking about something else, but in the meantime this little detail needed to be dealt with, simply that she knew more than I had told her and that was that.

"Beatriz Piazzola, like the musician."

She tapped the chair next to her with a pencil. Then we were both staring at the empty stage.

"I warned Marianne not to let strangers into a home, hers or anybody else's. But what can you do when children want everything to be so beautiful?"

She was Latin, but not from PR and not from Santo Domingo, with a soft accent and bad skin. Her English was shaped by a slightly British inflection, like someone who had studied in a grammar school with patient nuns, writing practice phrases in a small notebook, and presenting perfect papers. English had been part of her life for a long time.

"I'm working on a play right now, adapting a novel by the British writer Mary Renault. Do you know her?"

"No."

She smiled kindly as though my ignorance was nothing to be concerned about.

"It's the story of two women who live together on a house-boat on the Thames in the 1940s. They have lived this way for ten years, sleeping every night in the same bed and sharing, every day, their habits and imaginations. But they have never been lovers."

"Never?"

"No. Well, one night years before, but that is best not spoken about. They have, you see, a lesbian relationship but they do not know it. Enter, the American."

She held up one finger emphatically and laughed.

"Americans can provide the dramatic catalyst simply by entering. Because, for a foreigner, there is no difference between you and Hollywood. And, in fact, this particular American works in Hollywood. She eats lunch in the same canteen as Bette Davis. She is a walking movie and she is a lesbian. What's more, she actively pursues one of the Englishwomen and chases her into bed."

Beatriz was covered with ornamentation. She wore clashing scarves that flashed color when she moved and an extensive collection of detailed earrings, bracelets, and clips, a leather thong, and a wooden comb. It was all somehow just right and comforting because, if I didn't want to look at her eyes for too long at a time, there were perfectly legitimate reasons to look at the rest of her. If you watched Charlotte too closely she'd eat you up, but Beatriz was designed to be looked at.

"This affair, of course, provokes a great crisis in the friend-ship. You see, it forces them to confront the lie in their relation-ship and their complicity in that lie, a lie that has consumed ten years of their lives. Do you know what it is to have to relegate ten years to a lie?" The more involved the story became, the less expression Beatriz showed in her face. And I could see she was capable of great anger.

"I feel that way about my whole life," I said.

"Good. Then you know exactly what I am talking about."

"I've never heard of a book like that," I said. "I didn't know it could exist."

"It doesn't." She was laughing again, the kind of laugh you could pick out in a dark and crowded movie theater. "What I have just told you is my dream of this book. On the actual pages, there is no American. There is only a dreary man. And the secret, I'm afraid, is only the enlightened reader's imagination."

"Too bad, it would have been terrific."

"It will be terrific. We don't have to stop where the writer does. That is only the first step." She sighed then. "People will help each other lie all the time. Then they call it friendship, but it's not, is it?" I searched her face for the right answer but she gave me nothing.

"Little Marianne had no respect for what she didn't understand, and I lie to Charlotte that this is an acceptable invasion into my life, but it is not. I have given up many things to be able to love this woman, but I will not give up being treated with respect. I will not compoete for attention with a schoolgirl."

"Do you think she was killed by someone she knew or did Marianne just walk down the wrong street at the wrong moment?"

"Honestly, I haven't let myself think about it. I accept murder in general without question because the causes of such events are far greater than the individuals who carry them out. But I will tell you two things. First, people do not dump bodies of strangers in the river. They don't care enough. Strangers' bodies are left lying in doorways or in backs of lots. They are collected, half rotten, by the police and carried away in plastic bags. Then a report is filed under the title 'Unidentified Hispanic Male 20–25, Assailant Unknown.' And that is the end of it."

"What is the second thing?"

"The second thing," she said, jumping up from her chair, "is that we're going to build a houseboat in here and a gangplank. The lights will be so beautiful. White and hot at noon, the way the sun falls directly on your head and dulls the water. Then in the evening it will be midnight blue, cool and cold, the breeze coming in off the sea."

She looked right at me again, her eyes very full.

"I am not a monster. I am just a woman in all her complexities. We must be able to accommodate a wide variety of simultaneous feelings within the confines of our feminine bodies."

I watched her skin, primarily, and the way her wrists moved. She had the manner of inner grace and intelligent beauty that women only begin to realize in their late thirties. Everything is texture and wise emotions. It was in her voice, her gestures, in every habit. A certain familiarity with obstacles. She glanced, not fleetingly from side to side, but up and down, to herself and then back to me. Her eyes were deep and tired with wrinkles from the sides like picture frames. Beatriz's veins stood away from her neck and those thin wrists, so beautiful—there I could see every sorrow and useful labor. I got excited for the first time in a long time, realizing that this was in my future as well. Not just knowing her, but myself, becoming that beautiful. It had been too long since I had such hopeful imaginings.

"In this play, Charlotte is the abandoned friend, a woman who lies to herself. When you walked in, I was planning a scene in which every line is a lie."

"Is that the play you were rehearsing when I met you the first time?"

"Oh no. That was a silly exercise. Charlotte doesn't play naïve things. She must always be very frightening."

"She sure scares me," I said. "I wouldn't want to get on her bad side. She looks like she could smash a chair over your head, just like that. Like she could destroy you if it happened to occur to her or she had nothing else to do."

"No, no, no," Beatriz said, a bit too aggressively. "Anybody can destroy another person. Only, most people won't admit it. A good actress admits these things for us. That's why we love them so much."

Beatriz had the voice of a reformed smoker, bluesy with a cough in her laugh. She was skinny from way too much energy.

"Charlotte and I have been together for a long, long time. We have adapted to each other's failings. Charlotte has affairs and as long as she pays attention to me, I tolerate it. I do that because I love her and want to be together with her. What is more important to me than the category or theoretical concept of the relationship is that I love Charlotte the woman."

"Triangles are a big mess," I said.

"No," she answered curtly, as though I was misinformed. "Everything *can* work, but all the responsibility is on the new lover. A romance is always more exciting than a marriage, and a new lover has moments of more power than the old one because you are not so familiar with their bag of tricks. Unfortunately Marianne did not have the grace to adapt to the limitations of her role. The best newcomer is one with a great deal of respect. They have to respect me and they have to be considerate of me. Then we can all be generous and each one satisfied on some level."

She took a large bottle of seltzer out of a paper bag and poured it into two well-worn cups. Without the sweet shot of liquor that I was used to, it tasted sickly, like gas.

"My old girlfriend, Delores, she wouldn't be generous like that to me."

"Well, then you're lucky to be rid of her. Don't worry, she'll do the same thing to her new woman when her number comes up. Then you can rejoice. People never change their modus operandi."

That made me angry. It started in my upper arms, they began to ache. I got jumpy like I wanted to smash everything and scream at myself in the mirror.

"She just didn't love you. It's obvious."

I wanted her to shut up.

"You sound like you don't even care that Marianne is dead. You don't even care that someone squeezed her neck until it broke. Think about how scared she must have been. Don't you give a shit?"

"She was my rival. I have the right to be cold. Charlotte likes those young women. I can't stand them. I don't like them aesthetically. I don't like their skin. It's too easy to be gay today in New York City. I come from those times when sexual excitement could only be in hidden places. Sweet women had to put themselves in constant danger to make love to me. All my erotic life is concerned with intrigue and secrets. You can't understand that these days, not at all. Lesbians will never be that sexy again."

I wondered if her hands were too small to have fit around Punkette's neck. And then I asked a larger question. What makes a person suddenly able to commit murder? It's easier to hate than to kill, that's for sure. But I bet the combination brings the greatest satisfaction. When you kill the woman who took love out of your life, it can be an act of honor. But if you kill a woman because you saw her go-go dance in East Newark and wanted to feel her neck snap, then you too deserve to die. I marveled at how easily I accepted the difference.

11

THERE IS A limit to what you can do for yourself. When the mess you're in is too scary and overwhelming to possibly unravel, you have the choice to call in outside help. The best candidates are smart, compassionate, and creative. That narrows it down quite a bit. They have to have some free time, and finally they have to care about you a little. When I considered all the necessary qualifications, there was only one option: Coco Flores.

If everybody's got a best friend, I guess she's mine. She's always been a good talker but she learned to listen since she started working as a beautician. We met when she was managing an all-girl punk band called Useless Phlegm. Their name accurately described both their music and their personalities. When Coco suggested changing it to Warm Spit, they fired her. Then she enrolled in beauty school and got a job working a hair salon in the strip of new stores along the waterfront where the fuck bars used to be. Coco liked to hang out outside. She knew all the street people and they knew her. She knew the first name of every person begging for money between the park and the F train. "When someone asks you for money, you have to give it to them," she always said. "How can you say no? Dollars are best."

Of course, a beautician can't hand out dollars like business cards, so she developed a priority list which was topped off by two black dykes who regularly asked for cash. One worked the corner of Fourth and Second and the other stood under the scaffolding on Saint Mark's Place where construction workers had taken out a movie theater and were putting in a David's Cookies. They were definitely lesbians, Coco pointed out, and you have to take care of your own people first, so she saw them as her personal responsibility. There are more and more women in general panhandling on the street, but women asking for money usually plead. They cry or they will tell you what good reason they need the money for, like getting home to New Jersey. Not these women. They lean against buildings and talk to you real honey-like.

"Baby, can you give me a couple of dollars?"

Coco could get along with just about anybody and was, therefore, obviously unique. Somewhere in the background she was Puerto Rican on both sides, but they'd come over in the thirties so now she was more New Yorker than anything. Coco had never been a salsa queen but she did dabble in Latin punk and was always dyeing her hair a multitude of colors. But

Coco's most special feature was that she could talk poetry. She could turn it on and talk beautiful words that didn't exactly belong together but worked out all right in the end. Sometimes listening to Coco's stories was like swimming. You forgot where you were until it was over and then your arms felt freer. She'd read all the time, steal words for her spiral notebooks, and then throw them into one-person conversations that others could only watch.

"Hey Coco, isn't it a beautiful day?"

"I know," she said, flipping her chartreuse frost over her shoulder. "It's the gold-feathered bird."

"What is?"

"The bird's fire-fangled feathers dangle down."

We were heading toward the Hudson River, trying to get across the highway, dodging in and out of speeding vehicles, so I didn't quite catch what she said.

"The bird's fire-fangled feathers dangle down," she yelled over the traffic. "It means believe in the imagination, but it doesn't mean politically like you *should*. The words just do it by example."

"Where did you learn that, Coco?"

"My three o'clock appointment took a course at the New School. Next year she'll take two. She told me about it waiting for her perm to take."

In a minute we were on the dock, sunny and warm. I had a beer. Coco had an iced tea.

"Tell me a story, Coco. Tell me one of your great stories about some girl."

"Sure." Coco flipped her hair back and looked out over the water. It was almost pretty the way the sun brought out the blue and hid the garbage and dead fish.

"We were both up in the country at the estate of a rich faggot whose boyfriend went to beauty school with me. She was married and older but we flirted the whole weekend in front of everyone, although her husband, thank God, was absent. Finally, with big smiles, we decided to meet at midnight but forgot to say where. So I waited in bed lounging, making myself fuckable, wet, and sparkly. And, at the same moment, she was waiting for me, picking the perfect lighting and music, putting clean sheets on the bed. It got later and later, both of us waiting, wondering if the other would ever show. Finally, I decided I would not be disappointed and assumed my responsibilities as suitor by walking over to the guest house where she was staying."

At just this point in the story, Coco took out a nail file and started doing her nails.

"So anyway, the woods were dark that night, barely one star. Still, I found the dirt paths easily and walked them without a light, since my excitement was fluorescent. I was bouncing along, feeling the night when, right then, ahead on the same road, in another direction, a single spot shined my way.

"'Who's there?' she called out, knowing full well it was me coming to make love to her.

"'It's me,' I said. 'It's Coco Flores.'

"Well, let me tell you, it was fun. Everything was happening just the way it should."

"What did she say?" I had to know.

"She laughed and said, 'Oh, great,' and 'You're hot, you're really hot.' She said that to me because I was on her neck and scratching her fingers with my teeth outside in the woods. She held my hand in her leather glove. We were shy walking together in the night, but happy between kisses. During them we weren't shy at all. So I put my hand on her ass like it was mine. 'You are forward,' she said."

"Did you do it right there in the woods?" I asked Coco and then felt bad for the crassness of the question.

"No, we made it back to my floor, and I, being taller, younger, and the lesbian, unbuttoned her shirt until one forty-year-old breast showed with a nipple as dark as the eyes of Latin women. Do you know what was the most surprising? That she was so caring and willing to desire me. I was really touched, in that sexual way that leaves waves of sweet nausea that always end in the cunt."

Coco slurped her iced tea. She was really talking now.

"We enjoyed everything and kissed each other's mouths more than expected. 'Your breasts are great,' she said to me. 'Do all your girls tell you that?' When I went to her asshole, it was a cave inside a rock formation. When her fingers went inside me, they flew."

Coco got very quiet then, like she was feeling something dreamy and romantic, like all she wanted to think about was those fingers.

"You know," she said, "when you love women the way I do, when your life has been built around the pursuit of women's love, there are a hundred moments bathed in shadows cast from a fire or candle or the strange yellow light of an old kitchen. She was so tender with me.

"'So,' I asked, 'when was the last time you made love with a woman?' And she said, 'Eleven years ago.'

"At that moment," Coco said, "I saw her pain right away. It jumped out at me. I touched her face and asked, 'She hurt you, didn't she?'

"'Yes,' this woman said, so real. 'The woman I loved hurt me. She left me for a man. She was incredibly selfish. I wasn't heaven either, but she was incredibly selfish.'

"I touched her face like she was my baby, because she was so brave to have made love with me that night. I knew the humiliation she had been carrying longer than decade. I'd seen it many times before, across tables in bars, whispered in dark rooms and in the mirror."

Coco got sad for a moment and fixed her hair.

"So she looked up at me beautiful and naked and said, 'Women are so much easier to love than men,' and I wondered what would become of all this because I was so very deeply touched."

Then Coco was finished. She took a little bow my way and started chewing on her ice cubes.

"Coco," I said. "That was a great story. What happened next?"

"Her husband came up the following day," she said, sucking the lemon. "And that was that. Oh, she called me a few times in the city, but she wanted to run around street corners where no one would see us, holding hands and kissing. I couldn't get involved in a trip like that. I wanted to have sex in my life."

12

COCO'S STORIES HELPED me think through things. They were like therapy or hypnosis probably are. But as soon as I got home and was alone again, it was back into the real self. I couldn't get away from the sprit of Delores that haunted my apartment and clawed its way back into my mind. Every time I sat in that place, the demon took hold. The only thing that led me away from my pain was to think about Charlotte. Then I could forget who I was.

I finally decided that the thing to do was to ask Charlotte if she honestly thought that Beatriz could have had anything to do with Punkette's death. If she was guilty, I wonder how long it took her to plan the murder. What was the final blow that made her decide, "Yes, I will take this step now"? If I killed Sunshine, I wonder what would happen next? I'd probably just sit in the apartment waiting for the police to come. There'd be no need to run away. Where would I go? Why? They'd come and take me to one of the women's prisons and I'd have to wear green smocks, trade cigarettes, and learn how to play cards all day long with the other girls. When they bring you into court, is the press really waiting in a sea of flashbulbs, or does nobody notice, so you end up spending fifteen years in Bedford Hills taking Thorazine? Or, do you ever get away with it? Did Beatriz?

"You get used to the handcuffs," this customer told me.

She had been in Bedford for passing bad checks.

"'Cause handcuffs means you're going somewhere and somewhere is better than here. It's like a dog jumping around happy when he sees the leash."

I met her when she ordered an orange soda at Herbie's and sat there for an hour sipping it.

"All the girls don't feel the same about it. That's just my way of looking at things."

She had tattoos on her arm made from a blue pen and a pin.

"It gets pretty boring, so you look for little things to do."

They were straggly and uneven. One tattoo said "Danger" inside a heart. That was her lover's name, she said. Danger got out first but they never did try to meet on the outside. She told me that women who were there for murder, some of them, told her that right after you kill someone who really deserved it, you feel great. But right away you have to pay for setting things so right.

The couch was getting pretty dirty from me sacking out there every night, but I could not bring myself to walk into the bedroom because as soon as I stepped into the doorway, all of Delores's lies came back to me.

"I love you so much," she said. "You're my family."

Sometimes it got so bad that all I could do was lie there on the couch and watch the sky. If I had money I would have gone to a decent psychiatric hospital, but instead I was just another pathetic person on the Lower East Side. Charlotte and Beatriz were really my only happy thought. I hoped Beatriz didn't do it. Some people's passions are so unique that reality doesn't have the right to invade. That's how I felt about her and Charlotte in general—that they couldn't be measured by regular standards. They were exceptional. They'd staked out a means of survival on their own terms, working together to take care of things. I'd rather think of them that way, then there was something for me to learn that was positive, instead of growing into another dimension of anger.

There were bars on my windows and outside them there were trees. I could hear radios from the street and at night, the moon peeked out from behind the projects. Sometimes I got so angry I thought my teeth would break. The only other thing I could think of to do was go find Charlotte. So I washed out Delores's shirt and put it on again. It hadn't totally dried and was starting to look a little tired.

Being out on the street felt better for a minute because everything was interesting there and I saw different levels of pain and possibility in a combination that was somehow palatable, or at least diverting. It's only when you're open that the harshest thoughts pop right in. Delores and I, we had our honeymoon and then we had our crisis. That's when everything stops dead and you find out what the other person really thinks. It was that mundane. But all along I thought that if we could have stayed together through our little war, it would have been an opportunity to love each other in the most honest way. When you get informed, that's when the real loving starts. Now I'd have to explain myself to someone all over again. And, truthfully, there's so much confusion that the explanation seems to be an impossible task.

When I knocked on Charlotte's door, it was Beatriz who answered.

"Is Charlotte around?"

Beatriz stood there relaxed, wearing her little black stretch pants and red everything else.

"No, she's at her place."

I wasn't in the mood for any more surprises.

"Oh, I thought this was Charlotte's place."

"No."

"Oh."

"Do you want to come in?"

I stood in the dark hallway for one second too long.

"You mean this is *your* place?"

"That's right. Charlotte has a place uptown. Are you hungry? I'm just about to make some eggs. Is something wrong?"

"Nothing. I lost my breath coming up the stairs. Sure. Do you ... uh, mind if I look around?"

Everything was just the way I remembered it. There was one chair in the living room. The one I shivered on while Punkette danced. The tumor record was still on the stereo.

"Where did you get this album" I asked, holding up the jacket cover. It was a black-and-white photo of a French clone trying to look like a forties American movie imitating a thirties French movie.

"That's Daniel, my son. He thinks he's white these days and spends his money on these atrocities. Have you ever listened to this music?"

"Once."

"So you know it's terrible. I said to him, 'Daniel, this is bad music. It is worse than what you hear on the elevators in department stores.' But all he can say is, 'It's wry, Ma. It's pretending to be stupid. You'll get it someday, leave me alone.'"

Beatriz had a huge personality in that tiny body, and the difference between the two was quite clear. One was sharp and dangerous, the other, simply adorable. Like you could cuddle her until she got completely bored and bit your head off.

"The Gambino family opened a punk club down the block and he's been wasting his mind hanging around there with the moneyed youth. He is sixteen now and totally beyond my influence. Last year he thought he was Puerto Rican. Even *refugees* from Argentina think they are better than all other Latins. Especially Puerto Ricans. Did you know that?"

"No, I didn't. Is that how you feel?"

"Not here in New York City, the great equalizer, where we all become spics. Besides, I've never been a nationalist. Argentines are like Americans, master barbarians."

Beatriz started cooking up onions and scrambling eggs. She

kept talking with her back turned, so I could choose between looking at her body or looking around the apartment and she wouldn't know the difference. I kept my hands in my pockets and tried to see everything, looking for remnants of Punkette. I was so uncomfortable and tense, I felt out of control and needed to do something that made an impact. Just so I could be sure I wouldn't disappear. I walked around a bit in the tiny kitchen looking for something to hold on to when, on a whim, I stopped by the front door and quietly snatched the matchbook cover off the peephole. Then I had a secret too.

"My son is ugly to me these days."

The onions were sizzling on the broken stove.

"The more manly he becomes, the more I find him so ... unattractive. His face is too long. His skin is bad, like mine. He has no grace. The girls his age are so much more alive and brilliant. That's when I was the smartest, age sixteen. I knew everything I know now, but I didn't believe myself."

She could tell me anything. It didn't matter to her at all. I glanced, sideways, at the exposed peephole; it was huge. Beatriz was sort of humming and then she started laughing to herself. I was feeling nervous, sweating. She'd surely notice the hole in the door, then what would I say? She started to set the table, still laughing. What was she laughing about when everything was so serious? She looked up, suddenly, and caught me panicking. Then the door slammed.

I turned around expecting Charlotte's black eyes, demanding to know what had happened to the peephole. But instead, it was an overgrown teenaged boy.

"Daniel, why do you slam the door?" Beatriz said, knowing he was already in the next room.

Her son was homely and brash, filled with an authentic street cool of his own invention. His Nikes were laced, not tied, his cap was on backward. He had suspenders and wore his belt invitingly unbuckled. His style was too new and homemade to appear in any magazine. In two years it would all be mass-produced for white kids to wear, but for the moment Daniel was a happening young man. He was chill. He was fresh.

"Daniel, did you get the lock I asked you for?"

"I forgot."

"Well, don't forget again."

"All right, Ma, all right."

He was filled with an energy that could as easily become brutality as anything, and had inherited his mother's masculine nature, a woman's masculinity that is too delicately defined to transfer well to sons. He smelled of the future and that future was frightening to me because I couldn't imagine ever being ready for it. There was too much in the present that I didn't understand. He kept going in and out of the bedroom, looking at me in the eye once in a while. I noticed his huge feet as he was out the door again, back to the things that were really important: matters of power and honor.

Beatriz was quiet for three heartbeats and then resumed her faint humming. I looked for something to say.

"How do you like living on this block?"

"Too many junkies. They're even stoned when they rip you off. We got broken into but they left the stereo and took a cheap answering machine. Too stoned to steal properly. Can you imagine? Then, after a bit of time, they die. Probably only got ten dollars for it. Junkies sell everything for ten dollars."

Beatriz pointed to a dusty square on the side table where something had once been, something that was now sitting comfortably but underused in my living room. So Punkette needed small change and she needed it right away—or just wanted it, that might be more like her.

We sat down together at the table. Beatriz poured water from a clay pitcher and offered me good bread. She tore her piece in half and put it by the side of her plate.

"This neighborhood is a prison between C and D, Coke and Dope. You stay young in prison, did you know that?"

"No."

"In my country, I remember a famous criminal who had been sentenced when he was twenty and when he came out he was sixty. People gasped on the street when they saw his photograph in the newspaper because he stayed young while they'd all become old."

Then she grabbed my wrist and pulled up my sleeve. Her grip was like iron. Even though she was half my size, she was completely determined and in control.

"No, Beatriz, I don't have any track marks."

"Good. I hate junkies. They're liars."

"Well," I said, still feeling her fingerprints on my wrist. "Crack's the thing these days anyway. No needles, no marks, no AIDS."

She went to the mirror and started combing her hair, changing her earrings, changing her scarf. Her hands and feet were very tiny and her slippers, refined.

"Don't think that I'm afraid of death. It is the waste of time that disgusts me. In Argentina, I killed a woman, but it was a political assassination. I can say this freely, knowing it means nothing tangible to you."

I was eating eggs with a woman who said she had killed another woman, at least one, because she had to. Claiming it was almost as good as doing it, choosing to be known as a murderer. I wanted to be repulsed, but discovered, instead, a twisted admiration. Beatriz stretched her mouth tight, waiting for lipstick.

"Now a woman is dead who would have been murdered eventually and I have survived into this life."

I looked back at the open peephole.

"You in America don't have this decision but everyone else in the world must choose between making love and making history. You Americans impact on the world simply by eating breakfast, with so many people working so hard so you can have it exactly the way you like it. For the rest of us, we have to fight to affect anything, or else just live our private lives of hope and sorrow. If I want power in the world, then the world must take priority, not personal habits like love. At precisely the moment when I become convinced of which direction is most necessary to me, the other presents itself. Now, theater, that can be made for love or history."

"And now you're making it for love?"

She smiled a tired smile. It showed the beginnings of a

wrinkled face that would become increasingly exquisite with old age.

"I make theater with Charlotte. Sometimes in the early morning she is smiling, plotting in her sleep, being wild in her dreams. I brush back her hair and say, 'Bad, sleeping beauty, bad.' Because she is the mischievous imp in every fairy tale, and with a woman like that, all you can do is pretend. Those are the moments when I can see so clearly what we can make together. And you? What kind of family do you come from? What does your father do?"

"He's a narc in the Dominican Republic for the CIA."

"Oh, the intellectual type."

And we both cracked up laughing.

We were drinking coffee by that time and I could see right through the peephole into the hallway. It completely altered the apartment. It was staring at me, like Beatriz was staring at me. I needed another question, quickly, so she wouldn't look at me so hard.

"How did you and Charlotte meet?"

She was really solemn for the first time that afternoon, as though all this talk about murder and politics was throwaway chitchat but Charlotte was a serious matter. Beatriz's eyes were like the nipples on Coco's lover. Dark and sharp as swords.

"Onstage, of course. I'm not usually attracted to actors. In fact, they are my least favorite people in the theater. I could never say words I don't believe, not for money, or approval, certainly not for the principle of being convincing on any terms. Watch out when an actor tells you, 'I mean what I say.' That's the biggest lie of all. With Charlotte, the first thing I saw was her way of holding a script over her mouth so that only her eyes showed, laughing."

She illustrated her story with a napkin at the kitchen table.

"Even though it was hidden, you could imagine the mouth and how wicked it was."

Beatriz poured more coffee into my cup and I realized that I was beginning to slide. Maybe there was a bottle somewhere. If I kept drinking coffee, eventually it would kick in. I hoped that would be soon.

"In theater there are many moments inside of one moment, so without the precision of emotion, the play is nothing. It is slop. Charlotte and I were working together for the first time and we were developing a nuance that had to make itself understood in a matter of seconds. I tell you, she had me crying. She was wiping tears off her own face and slowly painting them on mine until they dripped down my cheek and onto my tongue. I know she's selfish, but she can fool the magician. She fell in love with me first, though, and I'll tell you why. It's because I'm not beautiful."

Yes, you are, I thought.

"Beautiful women never take beautiful women for lovers. They like elusive faces and quirky expressions. It's because they want to be loved for themselves, but they also demand adoration. And they don't ever want competition. Especially from the same bed. But, she unleashes me. Our first night together we had talked all evening, strolling the summer streets, with sirens and water pouring out of hydrants. Two elderly women were yelling in Spanish, their fat arms sticking out of cheap housedresses. When the time came to make love, I was sitting on my bed saying, 'Come here,' and Charlotte walked towards me in a moment filled with wanting and compliance. She took those steps across the dark room. She didn't look at me, but there was volition and desire and her body coming closer with no affectation. It was a raw honesty that showed me then how much the rest of my life was lies."

13

I WENT STRAIGHT from Beatriz's house to The Blue and the Gold and started drinking in a little booth behind the jukebox. When you begin to think about drinking and staying away from it, every dark street sends out a personalized path of light leading directly to a bar. It offers something to do, a place to watch the clock, and when you're drunk enough to sleep, you can go home. But, if you stay out of bars, there's nowhere to go but home, and then no place to go from there.

The news was on the TV but they were bombing Libya and I couldn't handle that. Then the channel got changed to the ball game, which doesn't interest me at all. I had to find something to think about in a stein of flat beer and a bag of Dipsy Doodles. When that's your evening activity, the beer goes down real fast and then there's nothing to do but buy another one. I was thinking about smashing Delores's face with a hammer, when I looked up and there she was. She was sitting at the bar, legs crossed, drinking a White Russian. She had dyed her hair bright orange and was bouncing her foot up and down in Sunshine's clothes, expensive and too big for her. There was a white headband wrapped around her forehead that made Delores's skin pale and her wrinkles deeper. She didn't look hip. She looked silly like Grandma Bozo.

I wanted to run out of there, but where to? Or run right up to her and scream in her ear, or flash Priscilla's gun, which was home in my drawer. I wanted to spit on her and break her neck and beg her to come back to me.

Delores was so close, I could hear her swallow. The sound gurgling in her throat made me nauseous. If I listened to the rain the way I listed to Delores's spit, I would have drowned right there in the bar. She was the woman with whom I had been living and loving, and at the same time a monstrous orange thing.

The day she left, I sat in my apartment, so sad. I didn't know how to be that sad. She was yelling at me and I just sat there.

"I'm leaving you for a woman who is going to marry me. You had your chance and now you just can't take it."

"I can't help it that I can't take it," I said.

What did I love about Delores? It was something concrete that she would do or say, it was how I'd feel when I saw her. She was always so happy when I came home and she liked being next to me walking down the street. She'd slip her arm into mine and say, "Oh, I'm so cozy." It was a sense of well-being above anything else. The problems started when she talked about "forever." My idea was that we stay together for as long as it worked and then something else would happen. You never know which way a relationship will go, so you have to be creative. I couldn't say "forever" unless I knew for sure it was true. But, I believed that Delores was my friend, so whatever changes we went through, we'd go through them together. I had a picture in my head where we'd talk it all over stage by stage and try this or that, always being considerate and in touch. I wouldn't picture it any other way. But, as soon as Sunshine came along, Delores split. Sunshine said "forever," so she wasn't interested in me anymore. It's not like we had stopped getting along or stopped having sex—everything was intact except the future. Man, was I surprised. I was so used to Delores being my friend and she changed so fast that I let her hurt me too deeply because I didn't know enough to treat her like a stranger yet.

"Delores, can't you just be nice and talk to me for one minute so we can figure something out?"

"You had your chance," she said.

See, from my point of view, Delores didn't play fair. When you dump your lover, you should show a little consideration to the woman you've been whispering to in the dark for so many nights up until that one. Not Delores. She took what she needed and then cut out. She was not sentimental. She was seasoned. Sometimes I thought Delores didn't know how to take care of herself, so she needed to find other people who would do it for her. If they didn't do it well enough, she'd get rid of them. After all, Delores was no spring chicken and you get tired of hustling. People like that run into a lot of lowlife and sometimes they become lowlife themselves. Her lover before me broke her nose. The one before that took her money. Both guys. Some nights I'd listen to Delores tell me about the brutality in her life and secretly I felt frightened, but I didn't know of what. Then one day I wasn't hearing about it, I was living it. It wasn't just Delores's stories anymore. It became our life together.

I remember one night we were walking home late along the avenue, both in suit jackets with girly decorations. We were both pretty. I looked up at her and said, "You know, I think you're my best friend, Delores." And she scrunched up her face in a kind of pure happiness you rarely get to bring out in another person.

"No one's ever said that to me before," she said. "That's what I've always wanted, a chum."

I remember watching her against the eerie glare of headlights knowing that I was the person Delores cared about the most. Now I'm the one she most wants to break. I guess that means I know her inside out. That's why I can't let go. Something organic keeps her right there, next to me. Whenever I move, she follows me because Delores left everything unresolved and that was a dirty trick.

Once, about two weeks after she left, I saw her across a subway platform in a crowd of people and she looked pretty, but seeing her alone and so close in that bar, she looked terrible. I've watched that face say so many different kinds of things. I'm afraid when I see her now because each expression is familiar and would evoke memories that, good or bad, I wouldn't want to be thinking about if we were to meet. I'd rather just be present. That Delores. I don't know what was missing, generosity or need, but that last day, boy, she was on a campaign of slash and burn. She was screaming at me, jumping around in a carnival of hate, trying to destroy everything, and I just turned off. I knew inside that there was no way to react that would have changed anything.

So when she came over and stood at my table at The Blue and the Gold, I knew I would be thrown into chaos.

"That's my shirt," she said.

"Hi, Delores."

"That's my shirt and I want it back."

She was holding her White Russian with its little swizzle stick. I didn't get up but I could clearly see her expression. It was blank.

"Hey Delores, where's your yuppie girlfriend?"

"She's not a yuppie, she's a lesbian."

"Okay, a preppie with a twist."

If I looked straight ahead, my face would have been between her breasts. She was wearing her black bra. I could tell.

"If you don't give me that shirt right now, I'm going to tear it off you."

I was thinking how, if she tore it, she wouldn't be able to wear it, but instead I said, "Look, Delores, why don't you call me later and we'll talk about it. Let's talk about it later."

One of the underlying reasons I said, "Let's talk about later," was that Delores had never called me since the day she left, not to give me her new phone number, not to pay the phone bill, nothing.

I got up to go to the bathroom and she kind of grabbed at the shirt, but let go before it ripped. When I got back, she was still standing there.

"If you don't give it to me right now, I'm going to make such a scene that they'll never let you back in this place."

Then I got scared. It wasn't losing the bar so much, it was the reality of the situation, of how Delores was angry that I was alive and she intended to obliterate me.

She yelled so loud, everything in that place stopped except the video games' repeating jingle.

"Give it to me now or I'm going to make a scene."

What could I do? I looked down at my table at The Blue and the Gold and slowly undid all the buttons. I handed her the wilted green shirt and sat there in my bra. You would think she'd at least leave at that point, but she took it back to her seat and sipped her drink. It was a while before Sal, the bartender, came over and told me to put on my jacket. That's when my head split open. It wasn't a headache. It was my skull. It cracked from the inside and nothing was keeping my brains together. I couldn't even cry. I couldn't do nothing.

14

ALL THAT NIGHT I lay awake in a dream of my own invention starring Delores as the phantom devil because no mortal being could have such impeccable timing. I dreamed I was wearing a white corset and it started to fill with blood. No matter how much I tensed my muscles, I couldn't keep it from seeping out. Finally the thing was soaked through and dripping red onto the carpet. I was in a fancy house with thick rugs and overstuffed sofas on wooden legs. I saw Delores coming and tried to hide the corset under the chair, but no matter how much I shoved it back with my feet, it kept poking out from behind the upholstery.

My insides were sweating as the sun woke me up. Rivulets of salty liquid ran and dripped under my skin.

"You'll be sorry," I told her to myself, twitching like a rough cut in an experimental movie. "I should just kill you right now."

Where the fuck was she? I called her old job but the receptionist said she quit. Then I took Sunshine's number out of the phone-book but got that fucking answering machine. I'm sure Delores was sitting there watching the color TV and screening her calls, that bitch.

"Bitch," I yelled, after the beep.

It was one of those days—cold on the outside but too hot under any jacket. I walked along the avenues realizing that all this time and after many incidents, Delores continued to ignore the state of my emotional life. The time had come to put a stop to this, to let her know how I really felt. On a whim, really, I bought a postcard of the Statue of Liberty and scrawled angrily on the back:

> I hate you Delores. I walk down the street dreaming of smashing your face with a hammer, but when your face was right in front of me, I had no hammer. What have you done that someone who once loved and cared for you could be made to feel this way?

And I mailed it.

By the end of that week my living room was filled with thirty novena candles. They were all on their fourth day of a seven-day flame. That way, when I would lie on the couch, there was a warm glow, sometimes feeling like a funeral, with me stretched out, open casket.

The walls were ghost dances from the inside and from the street, gyrating disco-heaven. If I crashed on the couch with fire all around me, it was more peaceful. I had something to look at instead of nothing and something moving beside me instead of no one. I was lying in state when the phone rang.

"Delores?"

"No. This is Charlotte."

I didn't make a sound.

"Beatriz and I just had a big fight about Marianne and I need to be with someone who cared about her. Do you mind if I come over?"

I looked around the apartment. It was a mausoleum. What's worse, Charlotte's answering machine was sitting on the floor right next to Priscilla's gun. I'd decided that morning that the two went together quite well.

"I'll meet you on the street," I said.

Since I slept in my clothes every night, I didn't need to get dressed. I just paced back and forth across the room, thrilled to the teeth. I wanted to see Charlotte in my house. The possibility of her being there made living somehow easier. I wanted to watch her crossing her legs on my couch, thumbing through my belongings with her big hands, tough and bony like the Wild West under a big sky. I wanted to see her engrossed, thinking something over and coming to an important conclusion. So I threw a bunch of towels over the machine and put the gun in the refrigerator, just in case.

I was waiting so hard that I almost forgot to breathe, and so got transported into a series of distant thoughts. By the time the buzzer sounded, I was in a dream in which I had become something frilly and lilting, like a Southern belle waiting for her gentleman caller. I descended the staircase of my imagination feeling like Scarlett O'Hara at Tara, but probably looking more like Norma Desmond. Or maybe I was one of those blonde creatures, a debutante at the cotillion drinking Brandy Alexanders, unconsciously garish in green eyeshadow. The drink left a frothy brown mustache that set off my wardrobe of various unnatural colors like beige or powder blue.

"Charlotte!"

She was sullen under the streetlight, her white skin luminescent in the night. My hero.

"When was the last time you changed your clothes?" she said. "You look terrible."

I watched myself grimy and wrinkled. Oh no, there were restaurant grease stains everywhere, baggy pants and the worst, light green socks with a pink shirt. How could I be wearing light green socks at a moment like this when Charlotte was just about to fall in love with me?

"Come on, let's walk."

She started off with a quick pace, leaping over the broken sidewalk with those huge legs. She was talking, but I couldn't hear the words. I was in my private movie and Charlotte was the star. In this scene, she slumped into her gait, in a hurried dissatisfaction, like the Irishman she was in cap and stooped shoulders, glum over his dinner. The grouse, though, was all appearance, for she was easily content. She could happily watch television every night and drink her beer quietly in a corner while the other men played darts. Underneath the coal dust, she was really a champion, a resistance fighter, a king.

"We've been at it all week. It's about secrets. I can't tell her about Marianne because she wouldn't understand. If she knew I'd had another lover, it would hurt her and yet, it's on my mind all the time, of course. So you must never say a word to her about any of it."

She passed her thumb back and forth across her mouth exactly like Jean-Paul Belmondo in *Breathless*.

"You see, Beatriz knows intuitively that something is awry. But she can't put her finger on exactly what. I mean, realizing that your lover had a sixteen-year-old mistress who had just been murdered is not necessarily the first conclusion one jumps to when there's mysterious discord at home. She doesn't know anything for sure, and I want to keep it that way."

She grabbed my wrist and turned it until my whole arm turned with it.

"Do you understand?"

"Charlotte, what are you talking about?"

I loved the feeling of pain that was taking over my arm. But as soon as she saw the pleasure in my face, she let go, and was sweet again.

"Beatriz is Latin. They have a sense of pride that is different than yours or mine."

She was lying. But she was lying so well, it drew you in. She had that expression on her face that some people use when they want you to know that they realize what's coming out of their mouths is rubbish, but they need you to play along so you do. Then it becomes your lie too.

"She would leave me in a second if she knew that I had been cheating on her. So if you ever have more than a cursory conversation with my lover, I hope you will be discreet about what you know."

There was some information I had that Charlotte didn't want me to disclose. But I didn't know what it was. One thing was clear, though; I had proximity to one of Charlotte's secrets and that's why she needed to keep me in her life. The longer I held onto it, the closer we would be.

"Do you understand?"

"Yes, Charlotte, I understand perfectly."

A long time ago, I learned that being alive meant playing by certain rules. Everyone knows that the specific choice of rules is an arbitrary one, but we agree on them to give ourselves something to focus on. One of the rules is that certain basic things—feelings, other people, and responsibilities—are real. When they slip away, the walls cave in and there's nothing left but anger at what you gave up along the way just to play along. Charlotte was the last thing I knew of that I wanted to believe in, because she had power, enough power to love and be loved and still be in control. So I loved her too, and let her have her way, even though I did know that she was lying.

"What did you like best about Punkette? I mean Marianne?"

"Don't deceive yourself. I did that out of pure vanity."

"But Charlotte, there must have been something about her individually that made you choose her. I know she was sexy and cute in a real touching way, without much passion. Was that it?"

Charlotte laughed, impatient at having to explain what was already so completely obvious.

"What did I see in her? The lack of pain. You can taste that on someone's skin. I like hope under my fingernails. You can smell it all day long like the insides of grapefruit rind. It's fresh and you think it can last forever."

I jammed my hands into my pockets. "But it's not forever," I said.

"Obviously, but who looks at a young woman and thinks of murder? I don't. Even if she was a junkie. A young junkie."

I only had to consider that thought for one moment. "No, I don't believe that. Punkette wasn't shooting junk."

If there was one thing I knew about, it was junkies. They're all over the place and you get used to them. They scratch their arms. They have nervous tics. They leave the water running and the fire burning. There's something very stupid in the way they glance around all the time. No, Punkette's eyes had no junk in them.

"Believe me, I was fooled too," Charlotte said. "But she started stealing things from my house and selling them. She took the television, the phone machine ... "

Right then Charlotte did the strangest thing. She grabbed my head with both hands, like she was going to kiss my forehead, but instead, she slid her palm over my eyes and held them real tight. Her hand took up half my face. Then she talked to me in a high, faggy voice.

"Can you see?"

"Of course not, Charlotte, you're covering my eyes."

It was quiet for a minute as I waited without struggling, until she started laughing and laughing and dropped her long arms, letting one swing a full arc.

"That's what my brothers used to do to me all the time ... "
she said, normal again and seemingly happy, still swinging that
arm.

There was something so brutal in her smile. She was a very
dangerous woman. She could really hurt me. And I realized that
I wanted her fingers inside me right then. They were long and
rough. If I was honest, I would have put my arms around that
thick neck of hers and climbed right on top of her fingers.

15

I FOLLOWED CHARLOTTE into the theater. We were the only shadows passing under the streetlights. The whole block seemed deserted and black.

She stumbled past the chairs and threw a few switches on the lighting board. Then the stage had two eyes, one rose, the other, pale blue. She pulled me by the hand until we each sat in our own spotlight.

"Wait a minute," Charlotte said, bringing up a soft backlight so I wasn't alone anymore. There was enough light for each of us and between us too. I looked up into the heart of the stage light and started crying real tears. Then I knew that was how they did it.

"Are you okay?" Charlotte said.

"Okay," I said.

"Great."

She clapped her hands and jumped up. That was the first time I saw how tight her ass was. She looked like a pressed flower lying in a book.

"Quick, this is our scene together, coming up. Sit at an angle so it looks natural to the audience. Okay: places, lights."

The lights were as cool as they could be, like the docks at night in a black-and-white movie. Charlotte was in character now, looking dangerous and interested. I was respectfully quiet, waiting for her to happen.

"What do you learn from examining me the way you do?"

She asked that question with a slightly British accent, as though we were guests at a turn-of-the-century garden party where the emotional dramas of the upper classes were carried out in the calmest and most naturally inquisitive manner. I could see Charlotte, parasol in hand, strolling the rolling green estate in a white afternoon frock and large hat.

"I like looking at you, Charlotte," I said. "Because you're beautiful and you change all the time. I like watching the changes, they make me happy."

I said that in my usual voice and usual New York accent. It was almost magic, like I was talking to a picture show and still being myself. I could be my own character.

She waited for a minute, tightening her jaw and stooping over slightly so her chin dropped and her face got longer. It stretched as her eyes died a little bit.

"Jesus," she said, slowly bending over an immigrant woman in Brooklyn somewhere in the days before the Big War. "Jesus, I've been beautiful my whole life," she said, wringing out the clothes and hanging them on the line between her fire escape and the O'Briens' across the alley. "I'm sick of it. People tell me I'm beautiful when they say they want something from me or they have nothing else to say." She brushed a wilted strand of hair off her sweaty face. "Beautiful." She was mocking now. "Beautiful as a spring flower."

"Not a flower, Charlotte," I said. "You're beautiful like a building with red brick and cornerstones. It took hundreds of men to build you and now you're solid and contain everything."

"Stop," she said. Then she screamed it. "Stop."

She screamed "stop" the way you yell at someone when they're just about to hurt you, so that when they do, your scream is embedded in their memory.

"Stop staring at me all the time, it's boring as hell."

For one minute I thought she might be serious and I felt so bad I wanted to say "shit" but instead I said, "Charlotte."

"You want to look at me?" she said. "All right, all right, goddamn it, I'll let you look. Look!" And she sat down next to me and waited.

I could smell her. She was almost rotten. I could hear her breathing and watch her chest puff up and down. I saw dirt in her ears. I saw a neck like a mountain and hands that were dangerous. They were murder weapons. Charlotte could kill me easily. It wouldn't take a thing.

"Let me see your legs," I said, and she lifted up her skirt. They were chimneys.

"Finished?"

"Yes," I said. "I'm finished."

So she became Charlotte again and turned up the house lights.

"There's that strange moment in rehearsal," she said, "where a good actor tries something new and it looks silly. Then all her moments seem suddenly transparent as though she's just a fake, not an artist. I love when that happens to me because then I have to start all over again."

Fuck you, Charlotte, I thought. *This is no goddamn rehearsal. This is true.* But I didn't tell her the truth. I hid it in a statement designed to contain both undying loyalty and bratty insolence.

"Beatriz knows all about you and Marianne. I didn't tell her."

"What did Marianne say about me?"

She watched me very carefully.

"Marianne told me that she loved you, and she really wanted things to work out. She felt lonely when she couldn't be with you. She told me some things that you like to say."

"Like what?"

"She told me that you said there was a palm at the end of the mind and it's on fire."

"Yes," she said quietly. "It's burning. And there's a bird. Its fire-fangled feathers dangle down."

"What?"

"Its fire-fangled feathers dangle down."

"Do you know Coco Flores?"

"Who?"

"She said that same thing to me just the other day."

"It's a famous poem by Wallace Stevens. A lot of people

know it. What else did Marianne tell you?"

"She didn't tell me anything else. Charlotte, I don't think I know what you think I know. I just don't think so."

She was sitting on her knees with her hands folded in her lap, looking like a middle-aged nun. She had knees like the man in the moon. When she knelt before me, they were as large as my face. I could lick them for an hour and still not cross all the mountains. Here's how I would make love with Charlotte. I would dress her up in feathers and have her hold me by the ass, carrying me around the room. I'd squeeze her waist tight with my legs and bury my face into the stone of her neck.

"Beatriz does know about Marianne," Charlotte said. "I just don't want her to know that Marianne was on junk. That's something Beatriz is not capable of understanding. Okay?"

"Okay."

I knew Marianne was not on junk.

"Can I trust you?" Charlotte asked, turning her head so fast her hair flew. "No, I don't think so."

"I'm sorry, Charlotte," I said, deeply ashamed. "Do you want me to go away?"

As soon as I said it, I remembered that that's exactly what Delores used to say whenever we'd have a little spat. She'd say, "Do you want me to go away?"

And I'd say, "No, Delores. I love you. We're just having a fight. It's no big thing."

I'd say that because I wanted to be able to persevere with people, to have faith in them. But I was so, so stupid. Thank you, Delores, for showing me how stupid I've been.

"Yes, I want you to go away," Charlotte said, laughing, as if she could have, just as easily, asked me to stay.

16

ALL THE WAY HOME, people were asking for money. Some were young, sane, and homeless. Some were boozers, stumbling in speech and movement with swollen lips and gray faces. Some were psychotic and poisoned. I believed every word they said. Each one wanted money from me. When I gave, I was blessed, and when I refused, they cursed me. I stopped giving then, just to see how many curses I could accommodate in one city block.

I didn't want to go home but I didn't know how to find anyone to talk to, so at least at home I could talk to myself. Sometimes on the street, waiting for the light, I'd try to talk to somebody but nobody wanted to except some sleazy guys. I got as far as my front steps when someone called out, expressly for me. I turned around and saw Charlotte, running to catch up. My eyes opened so wide and happy that the night came inside.

Oh God, she knows my name.

I was breathless and my skin began to burn with joy. She followed me upstairs and didn't mention all the fire around my couch, where we both sat, right on top of the sleeping bag and rolled-up towel.

"You know," she said, "it's wonderful to have a crush on someone but it can get frustrating when you can't do anything about it. When it's impossible."

That shamed me into looking down at the floor, and then was embarrassed for that, so looked at the wall instead.

"Do they always know about it?" I mumbled.

"They know," she said. "They know when you're sitting across a table and you want to kiss their neck. They can always tell."

"Well, if that's the way it goes," I said, "then no one's ever had a crush on me because I've never felt a woman kissing my neck across a table if she hasn't already done it in real life."

Then Charlotte looked at me and I looked at her. She let me look for much too long. She let me look at her huge legs with their beautiful bruises. Then she let me look at the skyscraper that was her neck. And I was so thankful she had taken the time to let me admire her like that.

"In my drawer are two nightgowns," I said. But I wasn't being sexy. I was being overwhelmed and looking down too much. "One is silky, light green. One is pink and frilly. They're both for summer. I pretend that different women come to sleep in my bed and we wear these nightgowns talking like high school girls and looking at the moon outside the window.

After we giggle and snuggle down cozy under the quilt, they run their hands along my bare skin and we sleep so soundly, with our arms around each other, that no dream can disturb us."

"Do it to me," she said.

"What? What do you mean?"

She looked like a maniac. She was strange.

"Charlotte? What are you doing? Are you acting?"

"I'm going to do it to you," she said.

I got so angry, I got so furious. Charlotte knew I couldn't have sex with her, I was too crazy. Besides, she had a girlfriend. I would never take love away from another person. What would be the difference between me and Sunshine if I did that? I could have punched Charlotte, I hated her so much.

"No," I hissed. My teeth were clenched so tight, my face was somebody else's face.

She slapped me. I was crying. I wanted to kill her. Where was my gun? Charlotte didn't kiss me. She pulled down my pants. She pressed her whole body so I couldn't move and jammed her hand inside me. I was pinned by a rock that was Charlotte. I didn't fight her. I wanted her. Tears and snot were everywhere and her breath was dripping wet all over my chest. Her fingers were huge and pried open the muscle. My body was the only thing left to me and now she was breaking that too.

I heard myself whimpering in a way that makes people despise you. Charlotte pushed and pushed until eventually she pushed me into a feverish clarity. I could see everything. I was burning. I could see that there was so much more pain than

I had ever imagined and I didn't have to look for it. Those closest to me would bring it with them.

Charlotte was sweating all over me. When she stood, the couch was wet and sticky and smelled foul. I couldn't sit up. I could feel her scratches, the impression of her grip inside me.

"Charlotte," I said. "You're just what I deserve."

But she was already bored.

17

EVER SINCE THE Rambo incident, Dino had been acting sort of hostile toward me. He smiled like he hated me. He was always saying how good I looked and how I should marry him. Instead of saying "Smile" every morning, he'd started saying, "You sure look healthy, Momma."

"Let's get married," he'd say about three times a day.

"I don't want to get married, Dino."

"Oh, come on, Mrs. Monroe."

He called me "Mrs. Monroe" because his name was Dino Monroe.

"I need a good wife."

"Good luck," I'd say three times a day. "Because a good wife is hard to find."

Charlotte had left three bruises on the insides of my thighs and she'd scratched my cunt so that it stung every time I pissed.

It was hard to walk around that restaurant all day because the welts would rub and then start to bleed.

"What's that between your legs?" Dino finally said.

I had to stop serving the blue plate specials and tell him straight to his face.

"Dino, be polite, man, because I want to like you. Be my friend, okay?"

Then he shut up for a minute but came right back to the marriage rap.

Momma was still doing her routine. But since she was too cheap to replace Rambo, she'd started working the register herself. Only she was practically blind, so she'd ask each customer how much the check was and how big a bill they were paying with. When it came time to go to the bank, she'd roll up the deposit in a paper bag and stick it in her girdle before waddling off. Theat's when we'd eat the corned beef.

One day, who comes into the place but Rambo himself. He was weirder than usual, unsettlingly calm. He had the collar of his jacket turned up and the visor of his baseball cap pulled down and he smoked Lucky Strikes very quietly, staring at the ashtray. None of the crew said anything to him. I had to talk to him, though, because I was his waitress.

So I said, "Coffee?"

And he nodded.

Herbie's is one of those places that rich people think are quaint and the poorest people are always welcomed. Anyone who can scrape together one dollar and sixty cents for the breakfast special will be served. It's not the kind of place that anyone gets thrown out of. Even if they can't pay the check, we just let them leave. That's what dive coffee shops are for. So no one thought to throw Rambo out. He just drank and smoked and thought things over.

"Look at that poor boy. He can't get a job," Joe whispered in the kitchen. I nodded. Most of the crew couldn't get a good job anywhere else. That's why they were all working at Herbie's. Take Joe, for example. Joe is a great chef and a good guy, but he's from Saint Kitts and he doesn't know how to read, so we have to pretend that he can. I put up all my checks with the orders clearly written, hanging on the line, and Joe stares at them all day long, checking back and forth every once in a while. But all the time I'm whispering, "Chopped sirloin, mashed, and string. Burger well, L and T."

Joe wouldn't last a minute in a fancier place. They'd get someone who knows how to read. He was right about Rambo. The guy probably couldn't find anything else and had to come in to ask for his job back. Joe bet me a joint. He'd get it too.

After a whole hour, Rambo got up and kind of shuffled to the bathroom. The back of his pants were dirty and stained. I could tell he'd been sleeping out on the street, really falling apart and punishing himself.

Rambo would have to hate himself and give up everything he believed in to crawl back to Herbie's and beg Momma for a job. She looked at him conspicuously over her glasses.

"You look like a bum," she said, too loud. "I can't take you back looking like a bum."

That did it. I would have done the same thing in his place at the same moment. I mean, I don't like Rambo, but to turn someone down before they ask, when they're just thinking about asking, takes away their dignity to make the decision to ask by themselves. It was unnecessarily gross. When Rambo blew his cool, he did the weirdest thing. He stared at Momma and then he turned around and jumped behind the counter. He leaped, like they do in basic training, and grabbed a big prep knife. He stood there, in battle, pausing for a moment to remember where he was and then plunged the knife into Dino's arm. There was blood everywhere. The customers started screaming and Rambo started running and Joe rushed over to Dino while Momma called the police. In the middle of this, I stood in the corner of the restaurant and thought, *Why Dino?*

Then I realized. It's just too damn hard sometimes to give up on somebody. Momma was his boss, telling him what to do for three years. All that time, Rambo had been phony polite to her every day. He couldn't let go of that. Somewhere inside, he thought he still needed her. That's why Rambo took it out on one of us. On Dino. On someone just like him.

Then I went over to Dino. His apron was covered with blood and he was looking old and shaking but he didn't say anything. Not even a moan or cry. He just tried to keep it all together by thinking about other things. The ambulance came and the cops came and when everything was cleaned up and settled down, Joe and me were the only ones left in the store. Eventually new customers started coming in again, looking for menus, not knowing about anything that had gone on before. So Joe and I looked each other in the eye, he heaved a sigh, and we started working again—me taking orders and him cooking them up.

18

SPRING CAN BE the best time in the city because it's so emotional, but some years it only lasts a day. This year it rained cool and gray for two weeks, which gave everyone enough time to think something over. But as soon as the sun came out, it got hot and that was the end of that.

I woke up that morning right in the middle of spring and it was too early. The sun had already come up but no one was taking advantage of it yet. Although some kind of breeze stuck its hand in through the window every now and then, it was obviously just a matter of time before the heat became unbearable.

There was nothing in the refrigerator except a beer and the gun, freezing away on the top shelf. I brought them both back to the couch and stretched out, naked, my skin so soft. All I could let myself understand on that beautiful morning, balancing a gun on my belly, its nose nestling in my pubic hair, was a profound sadness.

Everything was in confusion. A young woman was dead with no explanation, unless Beatriz killed her to defend her honor. But, was honor reason enough to kill a sixteen-year-old? If the answer was yes, it was certainly reason enough to kill a photographer from *Vogue*. Charlotte and Beatriz held a secret for me, but I couldn't tell if their answer lay in love or violence. Whenever one was apparent, the other stirred in the shadows. I could not integrate those two feelings into my life the way they fit together so perfectly in theirs. Charlotte and Beatriz maintain their passion and brutality with each other, but I have to face all my anger alone. Before the first hour of this new day had gone, I was already angry again, punching my fists into imaginary faces and hearing the echo of old lies. Then I finished my beer.

By late morning I was agitated and sweating and decided to go outside. On the street, people were moving very slowly. Some of them ahd been drinking already too, unusually tall, warm beers in brown paper bags. They drank Colt or Bud, a dollar eighty-five a quart. I could afford rum. I was working.

It's men, for the most part, who drink outside in the morning in the park. They sit placidly on benches with shirts hanging from their belts, nipples brown like roasted coffee beans, listening to a Spanish radio station. I wanted to listen too, but they started talking to me and I couldn't hear what they were saying. I just stared because they moved slowly like branches, like movie screens as the projector breaks down. It was like the last moment of a dream when the telephone rings and you desperately want to keep sleeping because you know there's nothing at all for you out there.

This bag lady that I know was looking in the garbage for deposit bottles. She had white hair and a thousand wrinkles. Her face was like crushed velvet, like you could peel it off her and she'd be young again underneath. It's too awful to be so old and sleeping in the shelter.

"Let me tell you something," she said. "Let me tell you something."

"All right, ma," I said. "What is it?"

"It's awful," she said. "It's awful when you ain't go no place to go and they put you in the street. To get a place, you gotta have a thousand dollars. How can I get that?"

She wore an old winter coat. She wore everything.

"I don't know, ma," I said, giving her two dollars, but she didn't move on right away.

"It's awful," she said, starting to cry from realizing the thousandth time that day how awful it really was.

"I know, ma."

I was crying too. It was so hot. But the whole time, it was like she was on a television set and I wasn't crying for her because there are people just like her everywhere you look. I was crying for me because I didn't know how to live in this world. I had no idea.

"Let me come stay with you," she said. "In your house."

"No," I said. I looked her in the eye and said no. I didn't even think of a reason why.

"Okay," she said. We weren't crying anymore. Now it was back to business. "Okay," she said, holding on to the dollars I gave her. She went on to the next garbage can and I had another hit of Bacardi.

19

WHEN I WOKE up from my nap, someone had snatched the rum bottle and I had a sunburn on one-half of my face. I was grimy from head to toe plus Coco Flores was standing right over me, taking notes in her little spiral notebook.

"You make a great metaphor," she said.

"Huh?"

"You look like a fucking wino. Get up. Come on."

She didn't lift me from under my arms, or even offer a hand up. She just stood there and told me what to do.

"Listen," Coco said. "Do you know that I like you?"

"Yeah, yeah."

It was embarrassing and I was still sleepy.

"Do you know why?" she asked, pointing me toward the water fountain.

"Why?"

I was really thirsty and then we washed up. I say "we" because Coco was standing there making sure I washed my neck and also my ankles, which somehow hadn't been washed in a long time.

"Because you see the world in a really individually twisted manner and so do I. If we don't stick together, one of us is going to get put away, and I don't think I'm first on that list. Do you understand? So don't lie around in the park like that. Any crazy could come along and smash a bottle over your head or spit on you."

Her hair was streaked magenta, lavender, and some other color.

"Amethyst Smoke," she said, fingering it playfully. "We just got it in the shop. Cute, huh? How many Puerto Ricans can you name with hair that's colors like Amethyst Smoke? Huh? That's really living."

"Yeah."

I felt like crying.

"Listen," Coco said. "It doesn't matter who Dolores was, why you loved her then, and why you hate her now. Delores is a hallucination, so the facts are irrelevant. What's important is how hurt you are. You're so hurt that regardless of who or what she is, Delores has control. In other words, you lost, okay? That's the reality of the situation. Look, I'll tell you the truth. I never liked Delores anyway. She wouldn't even ask me how I was doing, you know? She's not a friendly girl. There, does that help you feel better?"

"What do *you* do to keep it together, Coco?"

"I'm busy right now experiencing life."

"What's the difference between living it and experiencing it?"

"Now I'm seeing it with the narrative eye, you jerk. Take a look around. It's all there."

I started checking out the park with Coco, and it gave me so many memories of all kinds of people. There were winners and losers and gays and straights and me and Delores. There were too many dogs, though, and the whole place smelled of piss.

"Hey, look."

Coco pointed through the busted-up playground, next to the art gallery over by the condos where Cher was supposedly moving in soon. Two white women had been stopped by two white cops in one police car.

"Busted," Coco said. "Come on."

I followed her closer and closer until we were practically on top of the whole procedure. The cops were going though one of the women's pocketbook, taking out her personal things, and laying them on the hood of the car.

"Let's get closer," Coco said. "If they know that someone is watching, the cops won't try any brutality. They hate it when someone watches them do a bust. They lose their cool."

The woman being searched was definitely a junkie and couldn't keep a straight face. When he found a little piece of aluminum foil, she started jabbering away with half-baked explanations, as if talking as fast as you could would keep him from opening it. She was freaked out, scared, like she'd been inside ten times before and could not stand the idea of going in again.

Me and Coco were staring at the cop's fingers as he slowly unfolded the foil. He looked up once, looked right at us like he was nervous as hell. That's how close we were. He unfolded the first fold and he unfolded the second and then the third and then it was open. But there was no dope inside. No white powder, nothing. He couldn't believe it. He turned it over and over in his hand but there was nothing there. Then the woman remembered something. She started laughing and laughing. She remembered that she had gotten straight an hour ago and put the foil wrapper back in her purse. It was inside her, so he couldn't get his piggy paws on it or her. She was laughing really loud too. Then me and Coco were laughing and laughing. We all laughed until the cops drove away.

"Come on," Coco said. "It's time for the Hard Core matinee."

And still smiling, I followed her to the club.

20

SOME GUY WITH an Iron Maiden tattoo vomited in our direction as Coco led me past all the new condominiums and few remaining flophouses left on the Bowery. We passed the shelter for homeless men, the lobster place with singing waitresses, putrid Phebe's, and walked through the grimy doorway of CBGB's, the punk palace. The people inside were loud and overwhelmingly ugly. Each one had processed their hair into such an advanced state of artificiality that they deprived everyone else close to them of touching it soft or smelling it sweet. It was teased up, stiffed into spikes, shaved, extended, and always dyed, in a procedure utterly boring and out of date. Didn't they know that Sid Vicious was the stuff of Hollywood movies and they too would soon be petrified in their hardcore status if they didn't get hip to a new thing real soon?

Everywhere there were kids and the kids were making deals,

or imitating what they saw as the rough-and-tumble world of deal-making. Deals for bands, for gigs, for dope and sex. Deals that were nothing but big talk and small return. Deals because there was nothing else to talk about and the music was usually too loud to discuss anything substantial.

Also too many boys. Dirty boys trying to look mean, in training not to give a shit. Lots of boys in black boots, not a single one was pretty. The girls who hung onto them disappeared, but the girls who came in with each other were cute, chubby fourteen-year-olds with fake IDs, one shock of dyed black hair hanging over one eye. They were young enough to still be giggling from behind one cupped hand. Just like I used to do.

"See that girl?" said the sceevy boy standing next to his greasy friend. "She's an awesome fuck."

Then the band blasted again.

CBGB's walls were covered with remnants of torn-off posters. Thousands of little corners still Scotch-taped to the wall, and then some larger scraps advertising the Nihilistics, False Prophets, and the Spineless Yesmen. The air-conditioning worked.

Napalm was the band that afternoon. They all had the same haircut, shaved frontal lobes with backside shags that made them look like moles coming up through Astroturf. Their other common denominator was big, dirty fingernails that no woman should ever let near her body. Three of them had old underwear sticking out of the backs of their pants, which had been bought at a fancy Saint Mark's Place boutique years earlier when they were still NYU students. Now, though, the asses sagged, the colors faded, and their entire wardrobes were stained from Stromboli's pizza and puking. Phone numbers scribbled on torn Marlboro packs, learning how to smoke and drink, not enough love, just rock-and-roll bands with no personality, filled that room that afternoon. Two rums for me and then an oblivion of noise.

Coco and I stumbled out of there both drunk, since Coco was susceptible to influence and my influence was a bad one.

"Hey Coke, do you mind if I call you Coke?"

"Only if you let me call you asshole."

"Listen, Coco, there's Daniel, Beatriz's son."

"Who?" "My friend's son Daniel."

He was leaning against a car, looking as cool as a sweating teenager can look at four in the afternoon, deep in conversation with some white guy with dyed black hair.

"That's no Daniel," Coco said, leaning on my arm a little bit. It was one thing to be drunk in the air-conditioning, but out there in the sun it really took its toll.

"That's Juan Colon. Last year he was Juan Colon, at any rate. This year he changed his name to Johnny. He's from PR."

"That's no Juan Colon, I'm telling you." I really wanted a cigarette and started feeling up all my pockets and casing the crowd for a good person to grub from. "His name is Daniel Piazzola. He's from Argentina."

"No, man." Coco was looking for cigarettes too and pulled out two crumpled Virginia Slims from the bottom of her bag. "I know him. He's from PR."

Now we had to find matches.

"Excuse me, do you have a light?" I asked some gross shithead.

"Coco, talk to him in Spanish and listen to his accent. Then you'll know where he's from."

"What? Are you crazy? I don't speak Spanish. One, two, three cocksucker. That's all I know. Let's go to your house and smoke some herb."

But I had to talk to him. Johnny Colon, what a liar. Well, he came by it honestly, that's for sure. Charlotte and Beatriz created a legacy of lies and deception combined with certain elements of beauty that couldn't easily be discounted. But the closer I got to this gawky boy leaning against a car, the more clearly I could see the packages of neatly folded aluminum foil, wrapped in a rubber band. I saw how gracefully he hid them in the palm of one hand, making change with the other and always watching out.

"Daniel?"

"What do you want, C or D?"

"Remember me? I listened to your 'tumor' record. I've been in your house."

"Yeah? What for?"

It was really hot now, the car-hood metal was sizzling but I sat on it anyway because the pain kept me awake and kept my eyes glued to Daniel's.

"I knew Marianne too," I said, suddenly remembering the words of Urgie's sick bartender. "Her spic boyfriend. She said you used to watch out for her once in a while, even going to New Jersey some late nights."

I was very still while he made small movements with great agility and grace, the kind that can be used for baseball or sex or selling drugs on the hot cement.

"I liked her, you know, but she was a baby. She couldn't keep her opinions to herself and got mixed up in everybody's business."

"Someone told me she was a junkie," I said. "But I didn't think so."

"Who said that? Bullshit. Bullshit. Marianne never used except on holidays. But that's like everybody. Even the president does that."

"So what did she need big money for then?"

"She liked to eat in restaurants. She liked to buy new shoes at Manic Panic and get her hair done at Hair Space. She always bought the most expensive shampoo. She got messed up in too many deep things because she was a kid and never figured out who to say no to. Okay? Now leave me the hell alone."

I had to act quickly because my time was running out on Daniel's meter. He started to shrug his shoulders a little too much, like he really was tough and tough guys don't have time for too many questions.

"Charlotte said she was a junkie. It was Charlotte who told me that. I figured she should know."

Suddenly everything changed. Daniel stopped talking out of the corner of his mouth. He stopped making change swiftly with his right hand. He stopped acting like a man when he was only a boy.

"That's bullshit, man. You can't believe a word that bitch

says. Let me tell you something. If anyone's a dope fiend around here, it's Charlotte. When this whole thing happened, the first thing I thought of was that Charlotte got Marianne more high than she could handle and ended up dumping her in the water because she was too stoned to think of what else to do. That Charlotte is a real cunt. Don't believe anything she tells you. Okay, okay, you happy now?"

He jumped off the car with a jerk, as though I had upset him so thoroughly he couldn't stand to be in a place where I had just been. He started walking, troubled and slow, around the parking meter, easing back into doing business. Every now and then he twitched, eventually loping over to a third car, where he hitched his little ass up on the hood again and made change.

Of course it was Charlotte. How could I have been so blind? But never would Charlotte be part of something so sloppy and accidental as Daniel's scenario. I remembered those giant hands that would fit so perfectly around Punkette's neck. Those hands were the size of taxicabs. First they would stroke Punkette's hair, one hand covering her entire skull. Then they would caress her little breasts and slide between her legs, sloshing around in her wetness. And in that quiet, out-of-breath moment, right after she came, Punkette would look up, flushed and grateful, to see Charlotte's hands, with the same ease, crawl up her neck and break it without any effort at all. Without a thought.

21

"WHAT'S THE MATTER, you don't eat anymore?" Coco asked as I cracked open a fifth of Bacardi that I kept stored back in the apartment. "This place is a mess," she said.

I hadn't said a word all the way back from CBGB's. I wasn't thinking about anything either, except how to get drunk as quickly as possible. I really was too tired to think about Charlotte killing anyone. I didn't have the energy to strategize or negotiate or imagine. I was just beat.

"Still no stereo?"

"There's a radio."

She plopped herself down on the couch, putting her dirty feet all over my dirty sleeping bag.

"Any more books?"

"No, Coco, I still have one book. It's over there behind the candles. Buy me another one if it bothers you so much."

She stepped over a new wave of burning novenas.

"Think you have a future in mortuary science?"

"Don't be a drag, Coco. Look at the book."

She dug out the battered copy of Patti Smith's poems which I'd kept over since she was hot, and now that there are people who have never heard of her, that book is becoming harder to find. But thank God it is still available if you really need it.

"Show me the good ones," Coco said, throwing the book in my lap. "Show me the really great ones."

That was easy. The book just fell open to them.

"It's all about Judith. A woman Patti loved called Judith."

"But she's not gay," Coco said, completely relaxed. "She's married with a baby and living in Michigan."

"So what, she still loved Judith. Listen."

And carefully, I read aloud, knowing it would fill Coco with inspiration and happiness.

When all else failed: bird, magician, desert mirage, the prospect of gold and riches beyond the cloak and sleeve of marco polo, I attached all to a woman.

"More," Coco said.

Blushing monument: pink sphinx, sizzling squirrel. fallen pharaoh. the exhaustion of the mind which attempts to penetrate the mystery of her.

"More," Coco said.

I love her like the jews love the land. I love her like judas loved jesus.

"Yes," Coco said. "Yes, how beautiful. How wonderful. What joy in words. It's making my heart work overtime. It's setting my heart on fire."

"I know," I said. "I love Patti Smith."

We both sat there for a minute. Then I said, "Coco, tell me a story about a woman, a happy story."

"Okay," she said, flipping through the long-ago back pages of her notebook, looking at her messages and talking them together into a story right then and there. A story that never happened but would always sound true.

"The story is called 'This and That,'" Coco said.

And I repeated, "'This and That.'"

"And it's also about Judith. The same Judith that Patti loved, but years later. She came to my house. It was three o'clock. I left the door open and was cutting strawberries over the sink, listening to her climb the stairs.

"'Hello, gorgeous,' I said before she stepped in.

"'How do you know I'm gorgeous today? You haven't even seen me yet.'

"That sentence started out in the hall and continued through the threshold of the apartment as she took off her sunglasses and laid them on the counter with a bouquet of orange tiger lilies. All for me.

"'I love how they jiggle,' she would say later, fingering them, 'like breasts.'

"But at that moment she was still nervous, having come from the bed of her other lover.

"'I just knew,' I said, kissing her, being very quiet because inside I was thrilled. I was so happy that she had come to me.

"After some tabletop talk over tea and a joint, I could

embrace her from behind, naturally, because I love her so easily.

"'Relax, darlin', you can relax.'

"And for that moment, I felt her love me. For the rest of the day, though, I was never sure.

"We talked about this and that. It was interesting but what's more important, I was watching her. Then she said, 'Let's go,' and stripped to the waist like a sumo wrestler. We kissed, almost dancing, naked, feeling each other and the sun. It was so sunny and bright. Then we went to bed doing this and that.

"'When I was making love with you,' she said, 'I was thinking about Sappho and how her fragments are just what it's like. Everything wet for a moment and then something different like a rising passion and then something else.'

"She was lying in my favorite position on her back with both hands under her head, like a guy, really. It's the masculine things about her that I'm most attracted to: her gravel voice, her wiry arms, her thick black wristwatch. When she lies on her back like that and talks, I could say a prayer on her chest.

"Also, she's always thinking. Sometimes too much, but that's where I come in because sometimes I can be girly and help her relax. I can make her laugh. I know how to make her feel better. This is the Judith who is the woman who loves me in the afternoon."

"That's a nice story," I said. "But I'm really worried, Coco, because I think that Charlotte Punkette and I don't know what to do about it."

"What are you talking about?" Coco said.

"Daniel said that Charlotte is a dope fiend."

"Well, at least she's not a junkie."

"Why do you find everything so fucking acceptable? You know, Coco, some things are just too outrageous to let them go by."

"Like what?" She had on that insolent attitude where she could focus in and out of sincerity. I think she learned it from Useless Phlegm.

"Like fucking Delores," I said, really loud. "Like when fucking Delores said she loved me but she was really looking for a place to live. Do you think that's something I should take lying down?"

"Do you have a choice?"

"Fuck you, Coco Flores."

"Well, fuck you. Did you ever even ask her why she does what she does so you can drop it already?"

I saw that Coco couldn't decide whether or not to give in and let me say what I needed to say.

"Yeah, I asked her. I asked her why she said she was my friend and then didn't act like one."

"So what was her answer?"

Coco looked around for something to do and ended up lighting a cigarette and flicking the ashes on the floor.

"She said, 'I changed my mind.'"

As soon as I said that, I remembered the whole scene, like it was playing again on the video screen that sat somewhere between my mind and the back of my eyes. I remembered the day Delores said, 'I changed my mind.' She was sitting in the living room with a plastic bowl and a disposable razor, shaving her legs. I sat opposite her wishing she would cut herself. She was wearing green sequined hot pants and her legs were so white. I wished she would slit them open so I could watch the blood run all over everything like spilled paint. Her face was blank. It was the ugliest thing I had ever seen.

She left the bowl lying there, where Coco was now smoking. It was filled with little hairs. Then she put on some perfume and went over to her new girlfriend's house. I was stuck here with my nostrils full of Chanel. It hung in the air all around me and I had to sit and stare at that tiny bottle on the dresser, waiting for the scent to settle in my gut. I wanted to smash it.

"I don't understand you," Coco said. "You think normal people are running around killing each other and then you blame everything on Delores. You're just drunk."

Right then I got so angry I wanted to punch everyone. I was one of those people who talks to themselves and punches the air.

"Delores was a cunt," I said. "Sex with her made me sick. She always did the same thing. Whenever she wanted it, she'd pull her shirt up and bounce around, shoving her tits in my face."

"I don't care about you and Delores," Coco said, putting out the cigarette with her heel like we were on some street corner. "I used to but it got to be too much. You're sick. You need counseling. Here, let's talk about something else. Look at this fluorescent paint I bought. Hot pink."

I picked up the little jar.

"Let's paint my house," I said and smashed the jar against the wall so there was pink glass all over the place. "Let's slam-paint my house."

"You're too weird. It's not eccentric anymore. I'm going home."

"I'm going to cut Sunshine's face open with a can opener."

"Look," Coco said. "Your feelings are too large for the moment, okay?"

"Why?"

"Because everything in life is temporary so you have to live only for the moment and this is not the moment for which you should be living like this."

"No."

"What do you mean, 'No'?" Coco said, exasperated. "Yes! If you would believe in and be satisfied by what I just said, you would be a much happier person."

"No," I said. "It's just too much. I'll never give in like that. My anger is justified, therefore I need to maintain it until I get justice."

"Then keep on crying," Coco said, as if it was nothing.

I picked a little jar of green paint out of Coco's purse and threw that against the other wall so there was green glass too.

"Look," Coco said. "The first time was weird enough but the second time was sick because by then you knew what was going to happen but you did it anyway. That paint cost me eight bucks."

I didn't feel like saying anything right then. Not "fuck you" or "shut up," so I just sat there and Coco sat there too. Then she started braiding her hair. Then she left.

When the door slammed shut, I pulled out my gun from under the couch and held it, first in the palm of my hand, then gripped it cowboy style. It smelled like stale licorice or polished wood and it tasted like Delores. I decided that day that I would carry it with me at all times, until it took me directly to her. Then I would make Delores suffer. It was the only way that I could be happy.

22

ALL DAY AT Herbie's I wore the gun wrapped in a clean side towel, in the middle pocket of my apron. It felt great, hitting against my pubic bone.

Things were slow that day, so by three o'clock Dino and I were taking a break on the back stoop smoking his Kools, which he always pulled upside down from the bottom of the pack. We were talking about what kind of day it was and what those kinds of days reminded us of.

For Dino, it was about remembering being in San Francisco when he was young, "a few years back."

"It's the weather," he said, "that makes them all feel like that. It's like you're on vacation everyday and can take a bus in either direction. I had a friend, Max, who worked at the Do-City Barbeque. Eat Your Ass Off was their slogan. Old men be sweeping sidewalks anytime they got around to it because it's bright morning all day long. There's nowhere else I've ever been where you can take it so easy and still be in the middle of everything, except down south, but that's another story altogether."

I looked up, leisurely smoking, when I saw Delores coming down the street. Her eyes were glazed over all fanatic like and she moved as quickly as the Wicked Witch of the West pedaling that bicycle through Kansas. In her left fist, she was clutching my Statue of Liberty postcard.

I jumped up as fast as I could but she still caught me square in the chest.

"Don't think I care about your fucking postcard," she said, shoving me again with a strength I remembered immediately. I stood there with no expression and let her shove me all around the back lot of Herbie's. The gun in my apron was banging back and forth, cracking me in the bone.

"Don't think I care," she said. 'But everyone else is going to care a lot. I have some friends now, you know."

Well, the truth is, I never felt better. I felt successful. Delores looked so ugly that I didn't even have to shoot her. For the first time ever, she knew exactly how I felt. I had touched her. Delores finally got the message.

I watched her stalk away and picked up the beat-up old postcard she had discarded on the sidewalk.

"Shit, Dino, I mailed this months ago. God, the mail is slow. Man, it has really gotten out of hand."

Cocky as all hell, I delicately dropped it into the mailbox that was standing, conveniently, right next to the streetlight.

Dino was blinking, dragging on his cigarette, looking calm and very handsome.

"Funny," he said. "Funny how sometimes you're just sitting down having a smoke and all of a sudden you're in a movie. Right up there on the silver screen. And then, you're out of it again."

I was smiling away, feeling that warm spot on my chest where Delores had put her hand.

23

THE NEXT DAY, I made a big mistake. I started looking at old photographs of me and Delores. There was this one that really got to me. It was taken one weekend the previous August. We'd gotten shriveled and passive from surviving the city all summer, and when a customer at Herbie's recommended Ocean Grove, New Jersey, as not too expensive and not too far, we decided to stretch the budget and check it out.

About a half-hour after we got there, it became evident that the whole town was run by Christians and everything was closed by nine usually, and all day Sunday. Delores started calling it "Ocean Grave." The hotel that we were staying in was more like someone's home that got too large so they rented out a few rooms. In the foyer were born-again Archie comics and a board game called Bible Trivia. I remember that Delores and I pushed our beds together over by the window so we could see and hear the ocean. When we made love, we had to be quiet because we were scared of getting caught. But the next morning we took a little stroll down the beach and found out that one town over was Asbury Park, home of Bruce Springsteen and the famous boardwalk. We jumped in and out of that scene, playing ski ball, eating fried clams at Howard Johnson's, going to a rock-and-roll revival concert of the Marvelettes singing "Please Mr. Postman" for the seventeen thousandth time, and then we looked at the water. On the way back to bed, Delores and I crowded into an old-fashioned photo booth and took a strip of four shots. The first three were black-and-white with Delores sitting on my lap. But at the last minute, she grabbed my face between her hands and kissed it so deeply in front of the camera that my face got drawn into her face. When the pictures came out of the little slot, she snatched the strip right away, tore off the three posed ones, and threw them in the garbage, handing me the kiss.

"Here," she said, being nobody's fool. "I want you to have this one."

That's why I still have it and it hurts too much. Looking at it again made me realize what a pansy I have been, what a Caspar Milquetoast, letting her walk all over me. I conveniently turn to putty as Delores bops into my life for one second to cause total disarray and then she walks out of it again whenever she pleases.

That was it. There was no more beating around the bush. No more pretending. The time had come for me to take that step and get Delores. I walked around the apartment with my gun for a while. It felt good. What was more important, it felt natural. I wasn't going to shoot Delores and throw my whole life away. I was just going to scare her. Then she'd have to be polite for a minute or two. All I wanted was to say a few things to that bitch without having to hear her snappy comebacks. First, though, I had to get her into my house.

"Hi, Delores? This is me. I just wanted to tell you that I'm very sorry for any inconveniences that I may have caused you. I've thought it all over very carefully and I've decided that you are right and I am wrong."

I was talking to Sunshine's answering machine.

"Delores, if I had known that you were going to smash me because I wouldn't get married, then I would have married you. Being married to you could not have been worse than this."

I was trembling just a tiny bit.

"Well, anyway, Delores, I would really like to make things up to you in person. I would really appreciate it if you would stop by here soon and I could tell you how wrong I've been."

I poured myself a short one.

"Eight o'clock," I said.

Then I hung up.

The plan was in motion. The first step was to finish my drink. Maybe then I should reassess my plan. Maybe I should take the gun and shoot my face off as soon as Delores walked through that door. Then I had another drink and looked out the window.

"Everyone's a liar."

I was talking to myself out loud by this time and gritting my teeth. "Take Charlotte, she's as big a liar as Delores."

I hated her.

"'My house, her house.' Charlotte almost had me fooled into thinking she cared about me, that we shared a secret, almost like best friends. But the real reason she didn't want me talking to Beatriz was that Charlotte thought Punkette had told me something about Charlotte liking to get seriously high every now and again. In the meantime, there's that Beatriz looking for tracks on my arm when *her* lover and *her* son were probably high in front of her every single day."

I was getting ready to walk right over to Charlotte's place and give her a piece of my mind when I heard someone knocking on the front door.

"Delores?"

"No."

I opened it to find three women standing there. They looked exactly alike, even though one was rail-thin and the other two were not. Looking alike was what was unusual about them. Separately they would have looked very usual. Their hair was dyed the same color, black. And it was all the same style, ugly. They looked, at the same time, like a bad hallucination and very familiar. But I couldn't tell if that was because I was drunk. I couldn't tell which was more familiar, having hallucinations or them. Maybe they really did look like everybody else.

"We're from the Rape Crisis Center."

"What?"

"We're from the Rape Crisis Center."

"Are you collecting clothes for a thrift sale?"

"You have committed violence against women."

"What is this?"

I was not in the mood for this at all.

"You have threatened the life of Delores," they said in unison.

"We have evidence." One of them pawed a greasy, crumpled Statue of Liberty postcard.

"But I just mailed that yesterday."

"With the New York postal service, you never can tell. Anyway, you threatened to smash her face with a hammer."

"I didn't say I would smash her face with a hammer, I said I wanted to. It's not the same thing. Anyway, that's not the issue. The issue is who the fuck are you and get the hell out of here."

"Delores is a victim," the greasiest one said. "She is your victim. You are a rapist. You have metaphorically raped her."

"Why are you doing this?" I asked, almost crying.

"For justice," the skinny one said. "To get justice for Delores."

"Who's going to get justice for me? Where were you when I asked Sunshine to stay away from my bar on my night and she said, 'You can't tell me what to do'? Is that right? Where were you when I asked Delores why she said she loved me when she only wanted a place to live and she said, 'I changed my mind'? Where were you when Delores took my shirt off in The Blue and the Gold? Where were you when she was pushing me around Herbie's back lot?"

"We don't care about that," the middle one said. Her face was pasty-white and bloated, like she ate cortisone for breakfast.

"Why not?"

"Because your name is mud in this town," they all said in unison.

They each had their street names painted on their identical leather jackets: Dubble, Trubble, and Boil. Then I remembered where I had seen them before. They weren't from any Rape Crisis Center. They were Useless Phlegm. They were that horrible rock band that Coco used to manage.

"You're not from the Rape Crisis Center," I said. "Your names aren't Dubble, Trubble, and Boil. Your names are Debbie, Amy, and Lynn. You have the three most boring names in America. You're not social workers. Social workers drive Le Cars and carry appointment books. They really want to care. You don't do anything for anybody. You must really need bucks to walk around giving rape crisis counselors a bad name."

"Your name is mud," they said.

"What's the matter?" I said, walking past them and down the stairs. "No more gigs at the blood bank? Can't find any more health clubs that will pay you to hand out circulars? Couldn't find enough deposit bottles? Is that why you let yourselves be hired out as Sunshine's paid goons?"

"Why?" asked Boil. "Can you make a better offer?"

"I hope you got cash first," I said. "Or is she lending you her video equipment so you can make a music video of your band?"

"Video?" the one who wasn't skinny said. "All she promised us were free glossies."

"You are just bullies and cunts," I said. "Bullies and cunts."

"Your name is mud," they said. "All over town."

"Shut up," I said, slamming the front door behind me and running off down the street.

"Mud," they yelled after me. "Mud, mud, mud."

I ran all the way to Charlotte's house, but when I got up the stairs to the door, staring me in the face was that peephole. It was cavernous. I could have crawled into it. I didn't need to knock. The peephole would let me in. My palms left sweaty handprints when I pressed up against the door to look inside. The light was out in the hallway, so I stood, like a thief in the night, like a traitor committing espionage. I looked in and they were naked. Charlotte sitting strong and beautiful on a kitchen chair with her arms around Beatriz's tiny waist. They were sweating, their bodies glistening in the yellowed old kitchen.

Beatriz was curved and slithering, snake-like, looking down at the seated Charlotte with the greatest tenderness. Charlotte holding her so closely, her jaw relaxed, actually looking content. I could smell them from the hall. I felt great love for them. I became their accomplice. I would never betray them. Charlotte killed a lover with her hands and hid that behind a high while Beatriz covered it all up with lies so they could make love together in a tenement kitchen in the afternoon. Their lies enabled them to keep a passionate relationship. I was one of them now. I was so evil. I was in love with them.

I raced down the stairs onto the street, running, running again as fast as I could. My lungs were aching but I kept running, the gun bumping against my hip. My legs were sore and slapped against the pavement, but I kept running until sweat poured down my face and sliced my chin. I ran to Priscilla's house and she let me in.

24

I WAITED IN the living room while Priscilla got comfortable. She brought out a bottle of good vodka and a 1940s ice bucket with long-stemmed art deco glasses, pink. Everything was something. Nothing was regular. It couldn't be just a chair. It had to be tacky or exquisite or a great find. There were too many details, like coasters from various world's fairs and ice tongs from here and there and an overload of truck-stop ashtrays. But, bless her heart, that little dollface stepped out of the bedroom all dressed up for me, in her gown and panty girdle and even that black fall. She put on rhumba records and we danced around laughing and drinking from the bottle in between sloppy, drunken kisses. Then Elvis sang, "Wise men say, even fools fall in love."

That's when I murmured, "Don't be cruel," and fell on my knees at Priscilla's feet, burying my face in her polyester.

I rubbed my whole body in it. Polyster was my everything. I chewed on her girdle and she tightened the grip of tulle around my neck.

"I'm a terrible lover," I said, tonguing her thigh. "I'm the worst. You can still get out of it."

"I know you stink," she said, scratching eight long nails and two short ones under my shirt and down my back. "As long as I know the truth, let's just do it."

She put her hand on my thigh.

"Cool," she said.

She put her hand on my cunt.

"Feel how hot," she said. "You're burning up."

Pris tore off her Playtex and rocked back and forth over my face. So I ate her the best I could, which was like riding a bucking bronco, because she was not shy when it came to getting what she wanted. And there is little in life that is more terrific than being put in that compromising situation by a woman who outdoes her own fantasy. But then, surprise, surprise, Priscilla got all soft and dewy-eyed. That's when it hit me.

"Priscilla, you're the kind to fall in love immediately, aren't you?"

"It's true. I've never been able to kiss through walls or any kind of protection. That's why I need to carry a gun."

We lay back on the floor, quiet and out of breath. She raised herself up on one elbow and brushed my hair off my forehead.

"Honey," she purred. "What made you know I would let you in like that and give you exactly what you were looking for if you just presented yourself at my front door?"

"Well, Priscilla," I said, noticing her face under the makeup. "You're dangerous. You're dangerous and I'm crazy. We smelled each other in a rathole so I thought it might work. By the way, while we're on the subject. I'd like to ask you a favor. Take your gun back. I've got it right here in my pocket."

"Why, thank you, honey" she drawled. "But I have plenty. And not one of them is registered. Why don't you just keep it?" "I don't know."

"It comes in handy. And don't you worry about the address book. All that information is on my personal computer."

"Tell me, Pris, why did you start collecting firearms?"

She stretched out flat on her back to answer that one. Her breasts stuck up right into the air like the legs of a dead animal in rigor mortis.

"Years ago, when I was very young, I had a girlfriend who worked as a hooker. There were always creepy men coming around demanding things and she was very tough with them but sweet with me, real sweet. One night we were making love at her place. Her mouth was full of my breasts. She had such delicate bones, we were sitting together on a rocking chair. Suddenly, she stopped everything, right in the middle. I mean, both of our faces were flushed red. When you're that turned on, the air is sparking, everything could burn. So her pause had this magical feeling. I understood perfectly not to say or do anything. She picked up her gun, naked, with those sunshine stretch marks girls get from making babies, those marks were gleaming like gold leaf in an old book. She pulled open the curtain and a man was standing there jerking off. His dick was flopping up and down in his hands, like a sausage. I remember the steel of her gun and the precious metal on her stomach. And I remember his expression, knowing she would blow his balls off. But she didn't. He was some old boyfriend of hers and she forgave him. He left her alone after that, knowing that the next time she'd kill him for sure.

"'Get tough, cookie,' she told me. 'Get a gun.'"

"That's a great story, Pris. Do you know Coco Flores?"

"I've got more," Pris said. "If we're ever in a car for a long drive with no radio, I'll tell you six or seven."

"Do you honestly think I need a gun?"

I was moving real slowly, not sure of what I'd be hearing or feeling next.

"Priscilla, what would you do if someone you loved, who had hurt you very badly, killed someone you loved who hadn't done anything bad to you at all?"

"I'd stay out of it," she said.

"What would you do if your old girlfriend used you for a place to live and then dumped you for a yuppie in a loft in TriBeCa?"

"Keep the gun," she said. "You're gonna need it."

She dropped the accent and started washing up in the kitchen sink, putting on her plain clothes and looking like a normal girl again.

"I'm gonna give it to you straight. If you're nice, people think you're a sap. Give it back! Show how much you hate them. It's the only thing they'll understand."

"Yeah, what you're saying works theoretically, but in real

life, that's how people get killed."

"Oh, don't be such a pansy," she said, brushing her hair. She said it so carelessly that it tossed off her head with a stroke of the brush. I saw a fire inside her that cleansed her skin. It burned through her makeup.

Then I looked at the clock. The hands were dramatic. It was seven-thirty, almost time for Delores. I watched the second hand race round its face and I didn't have the stomach for hating her. I wanted, most of all, to believe in peace and love. I wanted to be romantic, read Chinese poems on a snowy day, watching a crow fly across a country sky. I wanted to sit with my lover in a big house in old sweaters, drinking tea and listening to Javanese music. I wanted to ride a horse and when it gallops, I start coming and when it stops, I keep coming. I wanted to be the horse.

"You're sweet," she said, kissing me. "And this was fun. Maybe we'll do it again sometime. But not too soon."

"Peace and love, Pris," I said when I walked out the door. "Peace and love."

And oh God, I really meant it.

25

THE BASIC OBSTACLE to getting justice is that everything in life has its consequences. Of course, you could argue that *they* hurt *you* and *your* revenge is *their* consequence. But bullies see themselves as the status quo, and when a person is a reactive type, like myself, what you consider "getting even," they call "provocation." They actually expect you to sit back and take it. And once you learn that the consequences are coming, it gets harder to ever relax. For each pleasure I've enjoyed I've had to pay back in sorrow. So now, every moment is shadowed by the evil one, waiting with a grin. Each emotion becomes, in that way, a parody of itself.

Outside it was nice and cool and clear. Every single person in the whole city was right there looking at each other. All the hidden craziness was blatantly dancing, blasting radios, making conversations, shrugging off responsibilities, flirting, fighting, leaving forever and turning over a new leaf. It was evening. It was beautiful. Then, across the street, I saw Sunshine.

I was a freight train. I didn't have to think. I ran right into her, screaming. Not words, but a high-pitched shriek and she saw me coming and was surprised. I ran into her face and it had surprise on it because bitches like that think they can get away with anything. They think they can take your girlfriend, rub your face in it, sic their goons on you and still be invincible. It was so sweet letting her know how wrong she was. I smashed her. I could smell her fear. I could smell her leather jacket, it was spanking new. I smashed her face and gritted my teeth and pulled her by her new shirt and smashed her again. I hit her so hard, my hand broke. I could feel it go. Then she actually fell down and began to cry. You hit them and they fall down. It really works that way. Then some blood started dribbling out of her nose, like a school kid. It was the same color as Dino's blood but there was a lot less of it this time. Everyone on the street who had nothing to do kept looking at us and everyone else kept walking.

She didn't say anything. I felt great. I felt really good. I walked away with my hand swelling but I started to feel tense again, so I kicked her one more time, really hard, and then I felt fine. I was so happy. I was free. I was the freest bird.

There was only one thing left to take care of, Delores. I touched the gun. I could shoot her. Or better yet, I could smash her too. I could smash her ugly little face.

Then the weirdest thing happened. I remembered the way Delores used to say my name when she came in after work. I remembered how I was the only one who never took her money or broke her nose and who always took care of her, even when she was driving me crazy. I remembered the way we used to run into the water in our underwear in front of everyone at the beach because neither of us had bathing suits.

Oh shit, I thought. *Oh shit.* I can't smash Delores. I love her. Maybe we can talk things over. Maybe she can act like a reasonable human being. But we'd have to go away from here, far away from Sunshine and all those yuppie influences. Then she could get her own apartment and we could have a normal relationship. All she had to do was show in some little way that she really loved me.

When I got home, the red light was blinking on the answering machine. Wow, my first message. I bet it was Delores. She probably thought the whole thing over and decided to come back home.

"Hello? This is Coco Flores. I want my eight dollars for the paint. Eight dollars."

She didn't even add, "I know you're having a hard time right now and I can't be there for you at this moment but I really am your friend." She just said, "Eight dollars." In fact, she said it twice.

I almost turned off the machine but there was a second message. Dolores!

"I hope you fucking die," she said.

All my breath came out of me. I was very quiet. The city was quiet too. All I could hear was the buzz of the cassette inside the phone machine. It was spinning around and around. What would happen to all my anger now? Where could it possibly go? I walked into the kitchen and poured a drink. I didn't care what color it was anymore. Then I stood at the threshold of the bedroom, staring at the bed. Maybe I'd be able to sleep there in a couple of weeks. I went back into the living room and stared at the answering machine, sipping my drink. I listened to the hum as the tape rolled on empty, empty.

"I just want you to talk to me, Marianne."

It was a man's voice. A man's voice on the tape. A man's voice was inside my apartment. He was panting, out of breath, but from tension, not exercise. You could hear him sweating. I punched the button and rewound it back.

"I just want you to talk to me, Marianne. Talk to me or I'll kill you."

"I know who you are."

Oh God, it was Punkette's voice.

"I know who you are and you're in big trouble."

Right on, Punkette. What a doll. Look at the way she stood up to that bully. Who was it, Punkette? Who?

But the tape finished.

All that was left of Punkette was her comeback.

Outside, the church bells tolled eight. I could hear the noises again, the cars and the drug dealers and people saying all kinds of bullshit. I was shaking with the memory of Punkette and the voice of her killer. A killer who wasn't a dope-fiend actress. Charlotte was just a run-of-the-mill liar in a standard fucked-up relationship. She didn't murder women. She loved and hurt them. That's all. She didn't kill Punkette. It was a man.

A man did it. Of that, I was sure.

26

"HI, CHARLOTTE," I said, when she answered my knock on her door.

Something about seeing her again made me happy, like I was the person I was supposed to be because Charlotte was in the same place as me. I rocked back and forth on my heels, shyly like a little boy in short pants and suspenders. I was smiling, feeling peaceful because Charlotte was as close to innocent as she could be while still being Charlotte.

"I was wondering when I'd hear from you again."

She looked great. She was so beautiful. Just the way gay men look when they're on display walking down the street, cool and embraceable.

"You can come in, I guess."

We sat around the kitchen table. I could smell an overripe mango fermenting in the heat, mixing with the warm garbage, the perfume of Charlotte's refuse. She was quite fashionable and proper that day. Almost pristine, like the librarian in the old commercials. Once she washes with Breck, she becomes a showgirl. She was wearing those trendy, nerdy horn-rimmed glasses on the edge of her nose, complemented by a shock of black hair hanging over her forehead. Her eyes were dancing black things.

"What do you say, Charlotte?"

"I say what the Maharishi said. 'The purpose of life is the expansion of happiness.' That's all."

We sat there for a while in the quiet. I broke it.

"You know what I found out? I found out that you didn't kill Punkette after all."

As soon as I said it, I wasn't so sure.

"Right?" "No, I didn't."

Charlotte was my fantasy so I could make everything right.

"And you're not a dope fiend after all either. You just like a little taste now and again. Plus, you do so like me. You weren't just trying to intimidate or get information. That's right, isn't it?" "Right."

"You're just a regular liar."

"I lie all the time," she said.

She took the mango in her right hand and bit into the skin. Then she pulled a strip off with her teeth. The whole world smelled of mango. It dripped on the table and when she wiped it up partway, she left sticky mango fingerprints for me to look at and admire.

"I'm always lying. If that's the truth, then what I just said is a lie in itself, which makes it even truer than any regular fact could ever be."

"Thanks, Charlotte. I was scared to bring all that up but I had to clear the air. Now we can really be friends. Don't you think? Now that everything is out in the open."

"Yeah."She was slurping the mango and untangling the threads of fruit caught between her teeth and the huge, hairy pit.

"One more question." I took a breath because my heart was pounding over this one. It was the hardest question of all.

"Charlotte, whose house is this really? Punkette said it was yours and you say it's yours but Beatriz says it's hers. I mean really, whose is it?"

"It's mine," she said. "Beatriz has a place uptown."

Then she laughed but it wasn't happy. It was unusually stifled. She looked down at her fingernails and for the first time I could see that she was uncomfortable. She didn't know what to do next. I didn't want that at all. I liked her on top. It made her radiate. It made her special. Some women you have to break through to get through to, but Charlotte was the kind to turn off if you got her number. It wouldn't be fun for her anymore. So I tried to put a stop to the bad feeling. I wanted to take it back so she could have fun again, but another way of thinking was rumbling and growing inside me. It was taking over before I had a chance to hold it back. I started to feel very angry. I don't know why but for the first time I really wanted to hurt her.

"So you're not a killer or a drug addict, you're just evil and a liar and I love you anyway."

I wanted her to stop me. I wanted to be generous instead of vengeful. I wanted to say, "I care about you," without trying to hurt her at the same time. I wanted to prove we were both better than Delores.

This is the place where the events passed very quickly. Time went so fast that even though there was a sequence, it was three-dimensional instead of chronological. Everything happened on top of each other at the same time. I'm not sure if it speeded up as I was speaking or right after I said, "I love you anyway." But somewhere between the *way* of *anyway* and the period at the end of the sentence, Daniel came into the apartment and he was sweating. I had time to smell him before I actually noticed him, but I'm not sure precisely when. I do think that before he said, "You cunt," I noticed that he was sweating and I noticed how much he looked like Beatriz.

"You cunt, you ripped me off."

He was holding a gun in his right hand, but I didn't see it at first because I was looking at Charlotte.

"This isn't a game," he said. "This is real."

She didn't have a chance to say much, but she did open her mouth. That I'm sure of. I saw her open her mouth but everything happened so fast that I don't know if she opened it to answer me or to answer him. I wasn't sure what moment she was in. Later on, it did occur to me that she might not have been in my moment or Daniel's but maybe just in her own as usual. Maybe she was about to protest Daniel's accusation that she had dipped into his stash at the wrong time, or maybe she was turning away in shame when he said, "And what about that girl, Charlotte? Huh, what about that little girl?"

Maybe she was turning toward me to defend her, to tell Daniel it was a man who did it, the man on the phone machine. Or maybe it was to tell me to leave, or not to love her anymore. That it wasn't worth it. Maybe Charlotte only opened her mouth to stretch.

Daniel's bullet caught her in the process of opening her mouth. It grazed the side of her head, but that mouth stayed open and she looked both ways out of the two sides of her eyes, behind those brown eyeglasses. She made a classically comic gesture like I Love Lucy used to make when she was in trouble. The laugh track would go wild over that one. Then she put her face on the table next to the mango peels because she thought she had been shot in the head and her blood was on everything.

The most unusual element of my experience of this event was that I hadn't caught up with what had happened at all. So right then I didn't have time to feel anything about blood from Charlotte's face, the third blood of the summer, the second blood I'd seen that week. I was still feeling the little seed of anger from our conversation and a bit of surprise that the way I expressed it was by saying, "I love you anyway." It was that emotion, I swear, that made me reach into my pocket and pull out Prisclla's gun. I'd held it, caressed it, and posed with it so many times that it felt natural, clasped between my fingers. Then I pointed it at Daniel's face. Of all the faces I had imagined at the other end of that gun, his was obviously the wrong one, but the turn of events had brought me to this place and there was no going back.

I felt a terrible explosion. Not huge, but compact and powerful. I tasted it in the air and then realized it hadn't come from me. It came from Beatriz, aiming at the sky. I knew I was able to kill someone, but only the right and most deserving person. I just had to figure out who that was.

Beatriz stepped through the bedroom doorway and slapped Daniel's hand, like he was seven. His gun fell to the floor, spinning, and we all watched it slide across the tiny room. My gun was still pointed at his face but Beatriz paid no attention. She held on to hers and picked his up off the floor. Then, with one in each hand, she fired them into the walls and ceiling until they couldn't be fired anymore and until the already cracked plaster fell off and you could see the rotting wood underneath that held the building together. Daniel was standing there surrounded by plaster. So was I. Charlotte was sitting, the collar of her shirt soaked through with blood. It was as though none of us could accept what had just happened, so we were all waiting for it to pass. But the room smelled bitter. It would never smell the same again.

I had begun the motions necessary to shooting Daniel in the face when, in the scheme of things, he wasn't clearly the most deserving. I had wanted to shoot him right in the middle of some thought that would have never been finished, had I been successful.

The face is everything. When you want to obliterate someone, you do it in the face. That's where all the lies come out. That's what you remember most about someone. No part of a person can be more cruel and stupid than their face.

Beatriz's face was stone with fury and had no room for surprise. Then she turned to Daniel and that all faded and transformed into the fear in every parent of burying their own children.

"I checked your arms for track marks every day," she said.

"Kids don't hit up that much anymore, Beatriz," I said. "They all smoke coke now."

"And you," she said, pointing to Charlotte, who was sitting in a pool of her own blood, unable to decide what she could possibly do about it. "You get out of my house and never come back."

"Your house?" Charlotte said, suddenly, as though she had nothing better to do than be indignant. "This is my house."

Oh God, they didn't know who lived there either.

27

IT WASN'T UNTIL the sun rose that I realized I had been up all night walking around and then sitting down in different places. Sometime during all of that I got drunk and some other time it rained. That's what I remember best, the rain. First, it started to land on me softly like kisses, and then it started to sing in an even, settling sort of way. It gave me something to do, which was listen to it, and a place to hide, which was inside it. Then there were thousands of drops coming at the same time and they started to roar, but I didn't want to leave, because it defined both parts of me: the outside part confronting the rain and the inside part that stayed warm and safe. I waited in the rain because it let me know that inside me there was still something alive that hadn't been ruined.

"Where the hell have you been?" Dino said through his teeth when I walked into Herbie's Coffee Shop and stood behind the counter.

"Huh?"

"You're a mess. Get over here."

He dragged me into the dishwashing section like I was a misbehaved schoolgirl and started running the water. "Shit, you got vomit all over your shirt. Where have you been? Never mind. Here."

He stuck my head under some warm water running out of those huge industrial faucets, and shoved a white T-shirt into my hands.

"Now, change your clothes and comb your hair. Here, use this." He handed me his red, green, and black Afro pick. "Jesus, now sit down and drink a cup of coffee."

I threw my shirt into the garbage and sat down in Dino's large one, drinking the cup of black coffee he put in front of me. The lights were so bright, you could see everything wrong and nauseating about the place.

"Do you realize that you have not shown up for work for a few days and you lost your goddamn job? Or are you in better shape than I think?"

A new waitress came whizzing by just then. She was old and had hair dyed silver and sprayed so hard it wasn't hardly hair at all.

"That's the Snitch," Dino said, chewing on a toothpick. "They hired her when you didn't show. She's always going over to Momma and saying, 'Dino threw out the crackers,' when I only did it because the mice chewed through the cellophane. Now you wait here until I get off and then I'm taking you to a meeting with me."

I sat in Herbie's for a couple of hours until Dino was ready.

The Snitch kept coming by asking if I wanted anything, being snitty 'cause I was taking up a table. Every time I said no, she clucked.

"You just leave her alone," Dino told her. "That girl is my responsibility."

I watched Snitch all afternoon long. I never took my eyes off her. She was a terrible waitress because she was rude to everyone she worked with. When she'd pass the busboy, she'd never say, "Excuse me," she'd only say, "Watch your back." When the customers asked what kind of soup there was, she'd say, "Read the menu." In between it all, she'd be clucking all the time and occasionally squealing to Momma.

Dino and I walked uptown from work. We had never been next to each other outside of Herbie's before and it was funny to see him out of uniform. In the sunlight I could tell that Dino got into looking like a cool, older black man. He wore soft green pants, tight around the ass, double knits with a little flair at the bottom over his two-toned shoes. He wore a tan V-neck sweater, a little tan cap, and lots of jewelry around his neck. He had a thin mustache that looked somewhat debonair, and a gold ring on his right hand.

"That drinking thing," he was saying, "all has to do with the twelve steps. It has to do with accepting a higher power no matter how you interpret it."

People looked at us once in a while as we walked. I guess we were an interracial coupe.

"I am over sixty years old," he said. "I woke up one morning and I looked around and realized that America is the land of opportunity and a smart man like me should be able to make a good dollar. So first, I stopped doping and drinking. Since then I got a mobile home in North Carolina, satellite dish, everything. I got a woman there and my son. I got another son in Detroit and I take care of him too."

He was smiling now, like he was on top of the world, like he knew the way and got joy just from telling me all about it.

"I do not take my worries home with me. I go to AA meetings, to AA dances, to the movies. But I make sure that when I hit that department store alone at night, I don't bring any troubles in there with me or else they sneak up behind you and take over."

I saw Dino three times a week. I wasn't some girl he could impress at a party. I saw how boring and hard his job was and how little he got paid. I saw him stumble out tired and frustrated, hanging around late sometimes like he had no other place to go.

"This is the meeting that I like the best," he said. "It's not near my house, but it's worth the extra trip."

The church basement in Chelsea was full. There were maybe a hundred and fifty people there and it wasn't even dinnertime yet. Many of them were black men.

"That's why I like this one," he said.

There was every kind of black man you could imagine. There were quiet gay men with skinny bodies, young turks with wild hair, old sophisticated intellectual types, businessmen paunchy in their suits, younger artists trying to get straight, and a whole contingent of street guys, smoking heavily around the coffee machine and asking each other for cigarettes. There was also a handful of Buppies in their dry-cleaned blah, and dudes like Dino.

Someone was talking. When he finished, there was a collective sigh and then a lot of people raised their hands.

"My name is Tom and I'm an alcoholic and a drug addict," said one good-looking young man, with an actor's composure and booming vocal tones.

Then everyone else said, "Hi, Tom," in a monotone unison, and then he said, "Hi."

Tom started to talk about how much he had wanted to cop that morning and how easy it would have been. When he finished, everyone raised their hands again and another guy started to talk.

"My name is Jeff and I'm an alcoholic."

Jeff was a bloated, nerdy-looking guy with thick glasses and food stains on his shirt, a typical egghead.

"Hi, Jeff."

"Hi."

Jeff talked about what his wife said to him the day before that made him want to drink and how much pressure there was at his job. It all went like that, being lonely or under too much pressure or not having a place to sleep or a bad memory. Whatever it was, they were all saying it and saying their names and everyone said "Hi" and each one had a reason why they wanted to get wasted and why they did or didn't let it happen. But after I realized how the whole operation functioned, I also realized what was different between them and me. They wanted to stop and I didn't. That got me off the hook real quick. So I stopped paying attention to the specificities of what each one of them was saying and got more into observing the atmosphere, like how each person talked as long as they needed to talk. Even if they started to ramble, nobody stopped them. Sometimes it got really boring but no one looked bored. I kept shifting my eyes back and forth between the yuppies and the street people. I couldn't help feeling that the businessmen were part of the derelicts' problems. But there was no hostility between them. Everyone was concerned with their own personal thing. There they were, sitting in the same room talking about the same topic, except that the employed brought their coffee in little deli cups and the street people drank the coffee provided by the AA.

I was leaning back, relaxing into the voices, when a white guy behind me started to speak. I wasn't paying attention at first but I could tell from his voice that he was white. It was in his pronunciation and the little sounds he made between the words. He got more nervous as he talked, clearing his throat too much and mumbling. Then he must have leaned forward on his chair because his hard breathing was suddenly on the back of my neck and it felt wrong. Something in his voice made my stomach get tight before I could realize why. I think my stomach heard him before my head did.

He's been having problems with his woman, he said in between coughing and other distortions. She didn't want to see him anymore so she cut out with no note, nothing. He knows where she's staying, though, and keeps trying to get in touch.

"I just want her to talk to me," he said. "Just talk to me."

It was the way he repeated the "talk to me" part that made my spine pull away from my back. He repeated it at AA exactly the way he had repeated it on the answering machine tape on my living room floor.

A kind of unfamiliar stillness came over me, the kind you read about in books when people reach the tops of mountains or hide from the soldiers or watch their lover leave forever. Sitting behind me was the same man who had put his hands around my Punkette's neck and broken it. It was the man who had carried her limp, light body through the projects and heard it splash into the slimy, shiny surface off the East River Drive. It was the man whose voice sat on a spool of cassette tape in a box in my apartment.

In my head was the sound of a waterfall that hit the rocks like a drum solo or a forty machine-gun salute. That's when I turned around and saw his long hair and David Crosby mustache, and his leather jacket with the worn-out fringes. It was the next-door neighbor from Charlotte's building. The cab driver with the electric shock on his door to keep the junkies away. It was the same man.

28

I WENT OVER to the coffee machine to get a better view. The killer had no neck. He was overdeveloped and sloppy. When he turned his head, I could see that his mustache was red and filled with spit. Then I gave him a general once-over with a degree of disbelief because my search for this man had taken me much too far.

I poured a cup of coffee. It was bitter. I added two spoonfuls of nondairy creamer and three sugars. Some guy was hanging out by the coffee machine being quietly but distinctly out of it. He kept talking in low tones with no encouragement from me.

"I've smoked some reefer and I got a headache," he said. "I've had a bad one since Saturday. I guess I'm out five dollars. A five-dollar headache."

I could see Dino checking me out from his seat. He flashed

me a big smile, convinced he had done his duty by turning me on to a really good thing.

"I've been smoking since 1964 and I ain't ever had no headache. It's them Trinidadians messing with the marijuana, putting in birdseed."

Dino waved at me. I smiled and waved back. David Crosby looked at the clock. His eyes were blue. He was a blue-eyed little boy.

"Used to be when it was in the hands of brothers, everywhere you'd go in Harlem the smoke was the same. No wacky bags then. No headaches."

Crosby was getting ready to go. He ran his large hands over his greasy hair and was out the door. I was right after him. I didn't say goodbye to Dino or anything.

Outside the sky was the kind of blue that only comes out when the sun goes down in early summer. There are days, now and then, when you're standing outside from the moment it starts until hours of beer and summertime conversation have moved the evening into night and that color into a midnight blue. Midnight blue has to be paid attention to softly if you want to see the blue. If you don't really look, it will seem black.

I followed him for three blocks before I noticed that at night I listen more and I also hear more as a result. During the day, the eyes take priority over the ears for me. Only when it's dark does the music come through. He walked with his head down. I walked with my ears. We heard a carpet of machine roar, plush in horns. On top were the voices, and in between were radios. Then he got into the driver's seat of his cab. I walked into the street and flagged down one of my own.

"Excuse me. Do you see that cab in front? Could you follow him wherever he goes? Thank you."

"Okay," said the Israeli behind the wheel. He had a Playboy decal on the windshield.

The thing about a cab is that you sit back in the leather like a movie star and instead of being part of the street and the life of the city, you only watch it. You don't come into contact. The only sounds are the sirens and the shrill whistles that bike riders blow when you're in their way. Then David Crosby parked in front of his and Charlotte and Beatriz and Daniel's building and walked into the hall.

What had begun inside me as a private disaster had played itself out so thoroughly that everything around me was also in ruins. Confusion and violence defined the world in which I was living, as well as the world that was living inside of me.

I took the pearl-handed gun out of my pocket and squeezed it between my hands. I pressed it against my heart and over my breasts, hard until my nipple was squashed flat against the bone. I passed it between my legs and in my mouth, in every secret part of me. I rubbed it over my face, pushing its nose into my cheeks, cleaning the trigger with my tongue. Then I was ready. Up the broken stairs, slowly at first, and then fast with no fear, stomping, tripping, flying down the stinking hallway. I slammed against the door with my fists first, with my right hand already gone from Sunshine's face, then kicking until my feet gave way too. So I threw my entire body against it over and over because I was the only person in this twisted city who wanted justice and was determined to get it.

I was fermenting in my own sweat. I was dancing in my own blood. I was panting, exhausted, looking for a solution in the limitations of my own body, when I saw his blue eye look out at me through the peephole. It was bloodshot and frightened, like he had been crying all the way home from AA. It was one eye with no context and no purpose. I put the nozzle of Priscilla Presley's pistol up through the eyepiece and then I fired. There was a nauseating whine, like a pig being slaughtered. Then the door began to shake. It began to tremble and I began to tremble from the shots of electric current. I was holding on to the gun. I couldn't let go. Electricity whipped through it and throughout my body, conquering me, making me part of the gun, part of the door, part of that rotting tenement building. The gun stuck in the door as I rattled and whined like the useless carcass of antiquated machinery. Like junk. That's when Beatriz came up behind me, pulled me away from the door, and pried my hands off the gun, which clattered, like me, to the floor. I experienced a physical manifestation of who I had spiritually been for the past four months. It started with that snowy night in March when I got a weapon from a girl in drag, and degenerated into this hot vomit called late July when everything is putrid in New York City. It was the numbest pain. It was a dull wound caused by some foreign power stronger than myself, which could dominate me whenever it pleased. I looked at Beatriz but she was watching the first drops of his bloody slime seeping slowly out of the gash in the door and sliding past my face onto the floor.

"I got him," I said to Beatriz. But I didn't move form the floor. I was completely exhausted. His blood was on the collar of my shirt. "I got the guy who killed Punkette. I made everything right. I suffered but I never gave up and now I have a victory, do you hear me? I have a goddamn victory. I won."

"What are you talking about?" Beatriz said. "You weren't going through all of this to find some man. You are just a lonely person who had absolutely nothing better to do. Don't fool yourself."

"Don't fool myself? You should talk." Then I remembered what was really important. "Where's Charlotte?"

"Sleeping." "Well, Charlotte is a goddamn liar, talking about fooling yourself. Everything she told me about you wasn't true."

"She did the right thing," Beatriz said. "Why should she tell you anything about us? That's private. Why should I tell you anything? I don't even know you."

I snapped my head back like she had kicked me in the face and cracked my head against the bloody base of the door.

"Are you all right?" Beatriz said without thinking.

I didn't say a thing. I wasn't even there. I was a floating sensation. A sea.

"Forget it," Beatriz said, disgusted by her own show of tenderness. "I'm not going to take care of you. Now get out of here before the cops come and it will all be forgotten eventually." And she went back into her apartment.

29

I LET MYSELF sleep for three days. During that time no police-
man came to my door to take me to prison. I had no bad
dreams. No person called my house to ask me questions.
There were no repercussions of any kind. A man went further
than the legitimate boundaries of human behavior and to the
extent that anything can be avenged, his crime was now neu-
tralized in the scheme of things because I had killed him. This
solved one question—the death of Punkette. There were many,
many questions that remained and which I had no energy or
ability to continue to try and solve. I could only ignore them.
I was not a satisfied woman. I was only quiet. And so, having
gotten away with everything for the time being, I sat up on
the fourth day and telephoned Herbie to ask for my waitressing job back. There didn't seem to be any alternative. By that
time, it was first thing Monday morning and he said to call

him back Tuesday afternoon for the final answer. So I walked to the park to wait.

As soon as I got there, I saw Coco looking around. I had the feeling she was looking for me. So I just stood there, not avoiding her, not running into her, until we ended up standing together staring at the graffiti on the bandshell, and the homeless guys who lived in front of it.

"Did you see the paper?" she said.

"No," I said. "Did the Yankees win yet?"

"No," she said. "They lost again."

"Figures," I said.

"Some guy on Third Street got shot in the face. His face got blown off."

We weren't looking at each other at all. We were both looking around.

"Yeah?"

"I had the feeling this might be important to you. I know you only read the papers when you're at work."

"It is important," I said. "Thanks."

Then we both waited.

"Listen," she said.

Coco very frequently began her conversational sentences with "look" or "listen."

"Look, I still like you. It's just that you've been too sad and it's hard to deal with that sometimes, okay?"

"Okay," I said. "I'll get you some new paints as soon as I start working."

I was quiet and Coco was kind of embarrassed so she said,

"Listen, I gotta go now. I have a ten a.m. cut and dye. But I'll see you later. I have a new story about making love in the bathroom of the Waldorf-Astoria during a drag ball. Imagine how crowded the ladies' room must have been."

I watched her walk all the way out of the park and down the street. It was hard to lose her in the crowd because her hair that day was canary yellow with lime-green streaks. I stopped looking as she was about to go out of sight because if you watch someone leave until you can't see them anymore, they'll never come back. That's a superstition but it might be true.

I walked over to the Polish newsstand across from the park and picked up a paper and a cup of coffee. Daniel was leaning on a parking meter wearing a baseball cap on backward and his name in big letters around his neck.

"Page eleven," he said.

"How are you doing?" I said.

"Same."

I started turning the pages.

"How's your mom?"

"Same." "How's Charlotte?"

"Still there. It's family, you know?" he said, flexing his biceps. I could see he was growing a mustache. "Family doesn't disappear," he said. "Family is forever."

"What does the paper say?" I asked, dumping it in the trash and sipping on my coffee.

"Well, that guy who got blown away?"

"Yeah?" I was watching him. We were so calm. We were both back in daily life.

"Turns out some girl went to the police a few months ago and tried to file a complaint against him. A dancer. He gave her a ride in his cab home from New Jersey one night and called her up the next day saying he would kill her. Turns out she ended up dead a couple of weeks after that but no one put it together."

He was so cool, he could have been talking about anybody. I could see that Daniel was becoming a man.

"How come nobody put it together?" I asked, playing his game now because I didn't have one of my own.

"Well, the paper says the cops wouldn't take the complaint. They asked her how she knew that the guy on the phone was the same as the guy driving the cab. They wanted to know how she could be sure. 'You talk to lots of men,' one of the cops remembered saying."

"What did she say?"

"I can't remember. Look in the paper."

I fished it back out of the garbage and turned to page eleven. I could tell Daniel was walking away, real slow. We didn't need to say goodbye.

"Men don't call me" is what she said to the police that night. "Men never call me." But the cops couldn't figure out what Punkette was talking about. They didn't get it.

I was so lonely at that moment, I have never been so lonely. I considered trying to remember every time in my life that I have needed comfort and someone was there to give it to me. But instead I walked back into the park and sat down on a bench watching the old people with their young dogs. I watched two skinhead teenagers trying to score and a man drinking wine out of a paper bag. An older woman was trying to explain something difficult to a younger woman and an older man and a younger man were in love. I saw art students in funky clothing smoking cigarettes and a straight couple having a fight. I saw everything because the sun was shining so brightly, the top of my head was cooking up a storm.

It made me cook up some very private things.

My moods swing like mad.

I feel close to people when I'm afraid of them.

Every person I've met, I've used as a measure to see what relating to people is like, how much I want it and how often it disappoints me.

It's all over, I thought.

I remembered everything that had happened and all I had to show for it was Priscilla's gun. I took it out of my pocket, wiped it clean, a nd wrapped it up in an old potato-chip bag sticking out of the garbage can. Then I tucked it under the bench, where someone who needed it could find it.

There wasn't anyone to be afraid of anymore.

At that moment, I didn't miss any of it. I didn't miss Priscilla and her polyester, not Charlotte and her power, not Beatriz and her desire. None of it was fascinating anymore. None of it was groovy. I didn't want to end up in any more go-go clubs or dirty theaters or smoke-filled bars or AA meetings. None of it meant anything to me. There was only one thing I missed. I missed Delores.

SARAH SCHULMAN is the author of sixteen books: the novels *The Mere Future, The Child, Rat Bohemia, Shimmer, Empathy, After Delores, People In Trouble, Girls Visions and Everything,* and *The Sophie Horowitz*  Story,* the nonfiction works *The Gentrification of the Mind: Witness To a Lost Imagination, Israel/Palestine and the Queer International, Ties That Bind: Familial Homophobia and Its Consequences, Stagestruck: Theater, AIDS and the Marketing of Gay America* and *My American History: Lesbian and Gay Life During the Reagan/Bush Years,* and the plays *Mercy* and *Carson McCullers.* She is co-author with Cheryl Dunye of two films, *The Owls* and *Mommy is Coming,* and co-producer with Jim Hubbard of the feature *United in Anger: A History of ACT UP.* She is co-director of the ACT UP Oral History Project.

Her awards include the 2009 Kessler Award for "Sustained Contribution to LGBT Studies" from the Center for Lesbian and Gay Studies, a Guggenheim Fellowship in Playwriting, a Fulbright Fellowship for Judiac Studies, two American Library Association Book Awards, and she was a Finalist for the Prix de Rome. She lives in New York, where she is Distinguished Professor of English at City University of New York (College of Staten Island) and a Fellow at the New York Institute for the Humanities at NYU.